# DOCTOR DEVINE

Nancy Devine took a post as locum to a country doctor, hoping to enjoy the rural life. However, the local people distrusted a young woman after their familiar old doctor, and the handsome young partner was apparently of the same opinion. Nancy fought to keep her patients, and to stay on good terms with her colleague and with her selfish young sister who occasionally descended on her. Despite setbacks, difficult patients and other crises, Nancy eventually found happiness.

*Books by Mary-Beth Williams
in the Linford Romance Library:*

WANTED — A WIFE
WARD SISTER AT ST. CATHERINE'S
LOVE HURTS

MARY-BETH WILLIAMS

◆

# DOCTOR DEVINE

*Complete and Unabridged*

## LINFORD
*Leicester*

First published in Great Britain in 1982 by
Robert Hale Limited
London

First Linford Edition
published 1996
by arrangement with
Robert Hale Limited
London

British Library CIP Data

Williams, Mary-Beth
    Doctor Devine.—Large print ed.—
Linford romance library
    1. English fiction—20th century
    2. Large type books
    I. Title
    823.9′14 [F]

    ISBN 0–7089–7975–0

Published by
F. A. Thorpe (Publishing) Ltd.
Anstey, Leicestershire

Set by Words & Graphics Ltd.
Anstey, Leicestershire
Printed and bound in Great Britain by
T. J. Press (Padstow) Ltd., Padstow, Cornwall

This book is printed on acid-free paper

# 1

NANCY DEVINE had been enchanted by all she had seen from the windows of the train for the past hour. Coming from the metropolis — and south-east of the Thames, where the scenery was not exactly idyllic at its best — she had passed through similar dark, satanic mill type landscapes coupled with high-rise blocks of flats marching into distances of town size, in the Inter-City train from Euston, and imagined most of her journey would provide such uninspiring outlooks. But after a British Rail tea, which she had enjoyed, she changed trains and the journey had slowed down considerably. Lancashire was not all mills, in fact only the south-east of the county seemed to be industrialized. There was a lot of demolition going on; she knew there was massive unemployment, but the train moved on through grey little villages, built from the limestone rock which was quarried from hills footing the Pennines, and after a couple of equally grey but sturdy towns, one with a magnificent castle dominating the scene, she had seen flashes of sea and suddenly all had been green and sylvan. Fat cattle grazed and there were dense woodlands, with trees wearing their autumnal yellows and scarlets; she actually saw deer in the grounds of a huge mansion and raced from one side of the carriage to the other as the train almost made a U-turn and then lumbered on.

"Never been 'ere before, Miss?" asked a rosy-cheeked farmer-type on whom she had almost trodden.

"No," Nancy smiled, "and I didn't realize it would be so pretty."

"Oah it's lovely round 'ere," came the rounded vowels of the native. "Good air, good milk, good food — "

"Yes, I'm sure. I get off at a place

2

called Carnforth. Do you — ?"

"Next stop," said the farmer. "Havin' a late 'oliday, are you?"

She was to find this interest in other people's activities indigenous to her new venue, and not at all intended to be offensive.

"No," she said with a little shrug. "I haven't had a holiday this year. Too busy. I'm a doctor."

"A lass like you — ?" The farmer was amazed. "That puts years on me, that does. Just qualified?"

"More than three years ago," Nancy confided. "well, this must be it. Carnforth. There should be a hire-car waiting for me. Thanks — " as the farmer lifted her three cases down from the rack and out on to the platform.

Carnforth, at first glance, appeared to be another Watford Junction. There were railway lines in all directions, but nothing much happening on any of them.

"The party for Greendales?"

Nancy spun around and there was a

peaked-capped figure regarding her.

"I'm to pick up a Dr Devine. That you, Miss? I didn't know it was a lady, like."

"Oh, there are quite a few of us in the profession, now, you know," Nancy said as she followed the hire-car driver out into the station forecourt. "Have we far to go?"

"Six mile about. 'Op in."

Nancy 'hopped' into the car and the busy-looking little railway junction was soon left behind as they drove down pretty lanes becoming thickly layered with the leaves from trees meeting overhead. Dense woodland lay to either side.

"Such a lovely time of the year!" Nancy decided. "You don't notice the seasons as much in London, especially in hospital. Mostly the thing that tells you what month it is is the type of flowers visitors bring. Daffodils can mean any time from February to April, and roses mean summer. Chrysanths — well, they seem to

4

cultivate chrysanths all year, now."

"You'll know round 'ere when's what," said the driver, confidently. "We can get quite severe winters and it'll rain after that, sure as little apples, before daffodils come. An' the daffodils come wild, under the trees, after the snowdrops an' crocuses. You don't need flowers in bunches 'ere."

"A real country practice," Nancy decided. "I'm going to enjoy these six months, I know I am."

There was silence as the car came out from the bower of trees and there was a kind of switchback for half a mile or so. The driver smiled as Nancy squealed at each bump.

"The kids love that," he said. "It's caused by natural rock formations under the road. The tarmac sinks but the rock never does. You know," he went on, confidingly, "I don't think Dr Wayne knows you're a young lady, like."

"Who's Dr Wayne?"

"He's Dr Gray's young partner.

You'll be taking Dr Gray's patients while he and the missus visit Australia after his stroke?"

"Yes, that's right, I've only corresponded with Dr Gray, who sounds a most charming old gentleman. I believe he's fully recovered by now and does right to take a long holiday. Unfortunately I couldn't get up a day earlier so I missed him and his wife. They were due to sail this morning from Tilbury, I believe? He never mentioned Dr Wayne. I didn't know there was a partner."

"Oah, yes. Dr Wayne's very popular and — and with it. He has a much bigger practice than the old man. I gathered he was looking forward to your coming. Said he hoped his new colleague played a decent game of golf and that you'd probably be discussing things tonight at the Royal Oak over a pint. I some'ow don't see you wi' a pint in yer 'and."

"Nor do I. It's been a long journey and I'll be happy drinking tea."

"Noa," chuckled the driver. "He's not expecting a female. By gow, I'd like ter be a fly on the wall when he finds out."

"How much further?" asked Nancy, thinking the conversation had gone on long enough. For years women had fought for recognition in the world of medicine as the equals of men, and proved themselves. She did not intend her sex to prejudice her work in Greendales, chauvinist male partner or not.

"We're 'ere," announced the driver. They had passed some magnificent houses standing in their own grounds and then driven through the village itself, with a large, chained-in green and a duck pond and pretty cottages covered with ivy and virginia creeper, a church with a square tower and a few shops huddled together and then a space where a huge silver crag overhung the road. Just beyond this the car turned into a long drive and the driver announced. "Crag Lee. This is

Doctor's house."

"I see. In the lee of the crag means in the shelter of the crag, doesn't it?"

"I suppose you're right. I 'aven't thought about it. I live in Carnforth meself. More goin' on, there. I'll see to your luggage, Miss, if you'd like to ring the bell."

The door was answered by a woman with a proud, pouting bosom and very shapely legs, wearing a tiny apron and with flour on her hands.

"Yes?" she asked. "Sorry, no surgeries on Saturday. Only emergencies."

"My name is Devine," said Nancy. "*Dr* Devine. I'm the new locum."

"You're — ?" the woman's face turned a shade of puce and mirth silently rocked her frame, "Are you sure?"

"Of course I'm sure," Nancy said rather sharply. "I've come from London and I'm rather tired, if you don't mind."

"I'm so sorry. Come in, Doctor. You must excuse me. Dr Gray didn't say — that you're a lady, that is. I suspect he thought it would be a great joke to play on us. Yes, leave the bags there, Mr Griggs. You have been paid, haven't you? Yes, well, as I was saying, Doctor, it's just the surprise of it. *I* don't mind a bit. Look at me! I was busy making pasties for a hungry young man, as I thought. I — I don't suppose you'd care for a meat pasty?"

"I should love one, with a cup of tea. I'm quite a hungry young woman, actually, so your efforts won't go amiss. My appetite is usually very good. You are — ?"

"Oh, sorry, Doctor. I'm the house-keeper, Mrs Waddell."

Nancy held out her hand, promptly, and laughed as they shook hands and then dusted flour off immediately.

"May I go up to my room and tidy up?" she asked. "Before I eat, that is."

"Certainly. I had put you in Mr Brian's old room — bachelor quarters, you understand? But I think you can have the big guest-room instead. It has its own shower attached. I'll take the big case if you can manage the two smaller ones. Well! I can't get over the shock, somehow. You're going to cause a stir hereabouts, I can tell you.

"I don't understand it, Mrs Waddell. I have just finished doing a locum job for a busy London doctor who'd had a coronary, and nobody gave the fact that I was a woman a second thought, so long as I knew my job. Before that I was in a hospital which employs the largest number of women doctors in the capital. Why should I be such a novelty here?"

"Well, I suppose we're a bit conservative in Greendales. Families have lived here for generations and we're green-belt, you know. There are no housing estates or anything like that. Certainly we've never had a woman doctor up till now. Now this is your room. It's very nice, isn't it? If you're to eat I must go and put my pasties in the oven. So have a shower and change, if you like. There's just time."

The shapely legs tip-tapped towards the door.

"Oh dear. I wonder if Dr Wayne knows you're a lady doctor? He's the junior partner, you know, and lives in the flat over the big surgery. He's very popular, but — " the dark eyes twinkled. "I'll leave you to it. You're very welcome," she threw over her shoulder.

"Thank you, Mrs Waddell."

Nancy wandered over to the large window and looked out. To her left rose the crag, looming darkly now that the light was fading fast. Ahead of her, beyond a neatly kept kitchen garden, was a valley dotted with huge boulders spewn up in some prehistoric volcanic eruption and — beyond that — greensward sloping gently to the sea. She was enchanted. Born in the Midlands and having trained and worked in London she had not seen much of the sea. Her mother had not been one for seaside holidays but

11

had usually sent her children, Nancy and her younger sister, Candida, off to stay with aunts and grandparents during school holidays, none of whom lived in memorable places.

It was now too dark to see and Nancy could smell baking. She drew the curtains, slipped out of her clothes and went into the shower-room where snowy towels were ranged on shining chromium rails. The water was softer than London water; she could tell as soon as creamy lather covered her skin instead of turning into scum as it did in the south. There was a towelling-robe behind the door and she hugged into it ecstatically, smelling deliciously of Pears' wonderful soap. She hadn't left a light on in the bedroom and was fumbling for the bedside switch when suddenly light flooded the room.

"Sorry, old chap," came from the doorway. "I tried to get back in time to welcome you, but we can chat later. I have to give you your patients' records and all that lark. I — "

12

Nancy threw the hood off her head and her blonde hair fell down to her shoulders.

"Oh, my God! Wrong room? I didn't know we were to have other visitors. Sorry!"

"Dr Wayne?" Nancy said, as steadily as she could in the circumstances. "*I* am Dr Devine. I rather think Dr Gray — for reasons of his own — has not broadcast the fact that I am a woman. I'm not apologizing for myself but I do think he has been rather naughty. Apparently I'm the first woman doctor ever to come to Greendales. Well, maybe it's time one did."

"You need to get dressed," said the other, coldly. "I have a dinner date, but I'll give you those notes about ten if you're still up."

"I'll be up."

The door slammed ever so slightly.

"Good-looking, his patients think he's God, and — I suspect — a woman-hater in the romantic sense," Nancy muttered as she dressed in a

13

simple blue wool dress and combed and pinned up her hair. "He simply oozed disapproval. I wonder if all Dr Gray's patients will disapprove of me? They could ask to transfer to *him* if they're all as suspicious of female medicos as I'm being given to believe. This isn't only a conservative area it's positively Victorian. I could be in for a bad time, here, and I was beginning to think it was heaven. Ah, well I'll go and eat. Things always seem better on a full stomach."

★ ★ ★

Nancy had partaken of two gargantuan meals in three hours, and felt the need of some exercise.

"Your dinner's ready, Doctor," announced Mrs Waddell, as the newcomer was examining the waiting- and consulting-rooms of her new practice.

"But I thought I'd had it, Mrs

Waddell. Two big pasties and treacle tart — "

"High tea," the other dismissed that effort. "This is your proper dinner. You're just a slip of a thing and if you have to work you need strength."

Nancy had followed the woman to the dining-room, wondering if she could take it.

"There! Quite light, as you see, Doctor. A nice omelette and damsons and cream. I'll clear up in the morning. My bus goes in ten minutes."

"Oh, so you don't live in, then?"

"No. I have my own home. You're not nervous, I hope, being alone in this big house?"

"Oh, no. I'm not a nervous type."

"Anyway, Dr Wayne's flat is over the surgery if you do get a fright. Coffee's on the hot-plate, and if you take a drink — ?" she indicated the corner cabinet.

"No, I don't. Maybe at Christmas — "

She had explored the big house. After all, the old doctor had told her to treat it as her home. He had told her to make her sister, Candida, welcome whenever she wanted to visit Greendales from the university where she was reading Modern Languages. The sudden death of the girls' parents in a car accident had caused an upheaval in both their lives. Nancy had had to be the strong one, make arrangements, find out how they stood financially, which was rather a shock. Their home had been heavily mortgaged and so had to go as Nancy didn't earn that much as a junior hospital houseman and Candida wasn't, of course, yet working.

"Where'll we live?" Candy had panicked. "Why have we no rich relations?"

"I've been inquiring," Nancy had soothed her, "and I can do locum jobs, which pay better, and give me a roof over my head as well. I'll only take jobs where I can have you with me. OK? That's while we catch our breath. Daddy's big insurance policy matures next year, and that's going to

16

provide the deposit on our new home. I think with my job I'll be able to get a mortgage for the rest and I should never be out of work. Eventually I'll try to get an Assistant's job in a big, prosperous practice, and save up until I can afford a partnership. By that time you should have got your degree and be working. OK?"

"I haven't much option, have I? I may have wanted to travel a bit and try out my languages for a year or so, but, no, I have to get a job. That's all I have to look forward to."

Nancy had looked at her pretty younger sister, so fair, with periwinkle-blue eyes and a soft mouth, at the moment looking sulky. She had been spoilt since birth by their parents, given everything she wanted, including Nancy's books and toys, which would soon be destroyed when she tired of them.

"Make allowances for your little sister," Mrs Devine had said when the youngster threw a tantrum, a

17

regular occurrence. "She only wants to play with your skipping-rope. She can't really skip."

"No," said the eight-year-old Nancy, jutting her chin, "and when she finds she can't she'll hit me with it. I can never do anything without her spoiling it for me."

"Now don't be jealous of your sister because she's prettier."

"I'm not." Nancy's hair had been fair and straight at the time, her eyes chocolate drops in a pale little face. "And she's not pretty when she screams like that."

But Nancy had always been expected to play the elder sister with as good grace as possible while her own childhood slipped away. Going out to play meant dragging Candy along, who seemed incapable of maintaining relationships with children her own age; and so Nancy took to staying in and reading, which made her very bright for her age and enabled her to pass scholarship exams and go to high school. As Nancy seemed well able to look after herself, Candy was sent to private school, and after that she boarded at Heatherdown to be made into a lady. Fortunately, she passed university entrance and played about for her first year, enjoying the attentions of male students and only working sufficiently to keep her scholastic head above water. When the tragedy of their lives occurred she was really frightened. All her life she had depended on other people, had wallowed in their admiration, asked and received, and now, suddenly, there was only Nancy and a situation which had to be faced where they found themselves as poor as church mice.

"We'll manage," Nancy kept saying. "Stop moaning."

"I've just lost my mother and father all you can say is stop moaning'?"

"Haven't I lost *my* mother and father, too?" Nancy snapped, her chocolate brown eyes filling with tears. "But I've got to worry and plan and *do* something about it. You could help by just letting me be still and think, Candy."

"Of course you can't get married to Barry, now?"

"No. I can't marry Barry, now. But I wasn't sure I was going to, anyway."

"Why? Have you had a row?"

"No, we're simply not so much in love as we were."

"Gosh! I don't think being in love is all that important. If a rich young man asked me to marry him tomorrow, provided he wasn't too bad looking, I'd leap at the chance and get myself out of this mess like a shot."

Nancy looked with a wry smile at her pretty, petulant sister.

"I'd be sorry if you did, Candy. That would be like leaping straight out of the frying-pan into the fire."

"Why?"

"Well, you'd be a wife and — and things would be expected of you. You know — ?"

"I love the way you grow all pink when we talk about sex. I say, have you and Barry ever — ?"

"No, we haven't."

"Have you — with anybody?"

"No, and I don't intend to until I'm really deeply emotionally committed, if ever I am. I think sex is trivialized, nowadays, and I'm not joining that bandwagon. You, Candy — " and again Nancy grew pink "you haven't, have you?"

"With boys? University students are just boys and fumblers. Like you I'm waiting, big sister, but not for the same reasons, perhaps. I don't care if I never fall in love, providing *he* adores *me*. That's what's important."

Nancy had been thinking and remembering the while she waited for Dr Wayne to return from his dinner date and give her the notes he had promised. She even slipped on a coat and took a turn in the moonlit garden for a breath of air. An owl hooted and then something gave a thin and final scream and was silent.

"I'll have to get used to country sounds. The quietude is almost tangible. I wonder if I'll ever get used to it after London? I wish that fellow would come so that I can get to bed. I *am* very tired."

She was so weary that once back in the warm house she began to nod. It was a quarter to eleven and she began to feel annoyed.

"I must have another cup of coffee to keep awake," she decided, and while she was sipping she sat at a desk and began a letter to Candy, telling her she was safely arrived and how pretty it was in the country. She didn't know how Candida would react to country life when she came to Greendales, but guessed it would not be favourably.

The letter written and sealed, Nancy's dander was really up when, at a quarter to twelve, there was a tap on the door and Dr Donald Wayne walked in with two file covers under his arm.

"How dare you!" was Nancy's greeting. "I had an appointment with

22

you at ten o'clock and now look at the time! I know I'm only a woman but I'm not an Aunt Sally for your personal scorn of female doctors! If I were a man I would — would knock you down for treating me so cavalierly."

Without using a hand Dr Wayne managed to move the pipe he was smoking to the opposite corner of his mouth.

"I take a bit of knocking down," he told her. "I'm six foot three and weigh fourteen stone and I've boxed a bit. A tich like you shouldn't make wild statements. Your talk of Aunt Sallies is lost on me. I had scarcely finished dinner when I was called out to a multiple car crash, and while I was trying to stick a few broken bodies together again, forgive me if I forgot all about you and our date. I have just returned from the hospital having seen our live victims made more comfortable and the two dead put in cold storage till morning. I do apologize, most humbly for the time and keeping you from your comfy bed."

Nancy collapsed like a pricked balloon. In her wrath she had felt six foot tall but now she was — what was it he had called her? — a five foot five inch 'tich' and feeling like a dwarf and very embarrassed.

"I'm sorry," she managed to almost whimper. "I should know these things happen."

The two files were placed before her. "National Health in that one and Private in the other. There's a map of the district you'll need to study. I am taking any night calls tonight and tomorrow, but as there are no DIPs at present we might both get our sleep. You can study those tomorrow morning. It *is* late now. Anything else?"

"No, thank you. Again I'm sorry for flaring up at you."

A grimace, which might have been a smile creased his features for a moment.

"I found it quite amusing. Very feminine. Goodnight." And he was gone just as she was concluding she could very easily hate him all over again for his final remark.

# 2

NANCY spent most of the following morning studying her temporary patients' notes from the files handed her by her colleague. She was still new enough to the job to find everything she read extremely interesting. Old Dr Gray's writing had obviously once been a very fine copperplate, but time had caused him to hasten his hand, though it was still much more legible than many doctors under whom she had worked. Also most of the case notes were neatly typewritten, and she had learned from one of many short gossips with Mrs Waddell that a young widow came in twice a week to keep the cards typed up from notes pinned to them, answer letters recorded on tape and send out accounts to the private patients. Thus she read of Mrs Mary Wainwright, a forty-three-year-old farmer's wife, that she had attended surgery on a couple of occasions complaining of an acid stomach. The treatment was recorded for acidity, and a note in Dr Gray's writing clipped to the card speculating on whether or not Mrs Wainwright should be investigated for a peptic ulcer if she came to surgery again still complaining. Nancy made a mental note to watch out for Mrs Wainwright. With all the goodies to be had on a farm it could be that there was too high fat content in her diet, and at forty-three the stomach couldn't withstand as much assault as when it was only twenty.

"Excuse me, Doctor. Coffee time."

"It's always some time, Mrs Waddell. You'll make me fat."

"Oh, go on! A slip of a girl like you. That's home-made shortbread. A Scotch recipe of my mother's. Don't leave any, now."

"Bully!"

Nancy was getting on well with

the housekeeper, at any rate. She hadn't seen Dr Wayne all morning but had been told he went out fishing or shooting, depending on the season.

"And what season is this?"

"Oh, they would be shooting. The butts are only a mile away from here. There could be a nice brace or two of duck in the freezer when I come in tomorrow. I did tell you, Doctor, that I only do lunches on Sunday? It's my half day off. That and Wednesday when there's no evening surgery."

"Yes, you told me. Er — if Dr Wayne is shooting and I get an emergency call for him, what do I do?"

"Well, he's left a phone number on the pad. But it may never happen, eh? If the house is ever left, you notify the telephone people and they pass on calls to the medical practice in town. There's always somebody on call. I do think this afternoon you should try out Doctor's car and drive around with your map. There's as much as a mile between farms, *and* three villages to cover."

"Yes, I will, Mrs Waddell."

This conversation had taken place while she was eating her breakfast. She now sipped coffee and read about General Yates, an octogenarian with hypertension who had withstood a couple of strokes despite the twin sins of drinking and smoking. From him to another widower of only thirty-two, George Barclay, estate manager to the Huntleys of the Hall. He had a small daughter of only three. 'Neurosis caused by domestic difficulties, no doubt,' Dr Gray had penned. 'Complains of insomnia. No treatment recommended.' The small daughter, Deborah, also had quite a spate of visits on her card. 'Persistent irritating cough. No inflammation of bronchial tract. Nervous in origin?' 'Refuses to eat regularly. Small child but appears healthy. Suggested no sweets and small, simple meals.' The sixth entry

29

made Nancy sit up rigidly. 'Greenstick fracture of right humerus. Much bruising. Set in hospital, and healed well.'

"Now how did that happen?" Nancy asked herself. There was always this nagging fear that a parent, irritated beyond endurance, had caused the injury. They could go momentarily berserk and a three-year-old child was so small and easily damaged. She pondered on George Barclay's earlier mentioned domestic difficulties. Who looked after Deborah while he was working? She made a mental note to find time to visit George, in the near future. 'Just getting to know all my patients,' would be as good an excuse as any.

She could hear the phone ringing in the hall and Mrs Waddell's answering voice as she was glancing through a list headed 'Monthly home visits required due to age or disability. Arrange for prescriptions to be delivered. Be prepared to listen sympathetically.'

"Doctor wrote that specially for me,"

Nancy decided. "The handwriting is quite fresh."

"Dr Devine — ?" Mrs Waddell stood in the doorway, looking rather flustered, her splendid bosom in a peach-satin blouse rising and falling quickly. "I can't reach Dr Wayne and there's an emergency. You see what comes of talking of the devil — ?"

"Well, what is it?"

"Young Jimmy Spence has swallowed a bone, and his mother says it's stuck and he's choking."

"Get them on the phone, would you please?"

"Yes, Doctor. Won't be a tick. There you are."

"Mrs Spence?" Nancy said to the frightened parent. "My name is Devine and I'm a qualified doctor. Now tell me what kind of bone Johnny has swallowed. Part of a pork chop? Then it's probably splintered and must be painful. Can you get him to relax? He's probably trying to swallow and causing the choking sensation. Assure him it'll be all right. Have you a car? Good! His father's home? Well, please wrap Johnny up well and bring him over to surgery. Why can't I come to you? Well, I have all the necessary equipment here, for one thing, and it would take me as long to get to you as you to come here. I can start getting everything ready for your arrival if you'll just do as I say. Tell Johnny it will be all right and not to try to swallow."

"Can you help me set up for a tracheotomy just in case, Mrs Waddell?" she then asked. "It may not be necessary but better to be sure than sorry. You can tell me where everything is and I'll sterilize some instruments and scrub up."

By the time the twelve-year-old patient arrived he was cold and shocked but able to walk into the consulting-room. The parents were asked to wait outside.

"Now, Johnny," Nancy said, helping the lad on to the examination couch. "I want you to be very good although I know you feel very uncomfortable and frightened. Just do as I say. First of all, mouth wide open — ah! I can see the bone. It's lying crossways — no wonder it wouldn't go down. Now I think I can get some long tweezers on to it, and when I do we're home and dry. The worst part is getting the tweezers down there, because I can't give you anything to make you relax in case the bone slips further. We don't want that, do we? You'll want like mad to retch while I'm poking about, but if you say to yourself 'Johnny relax. Re-lax,' then maybe you can control yourself long enough for me to get a hold. Once that happens I have a hypodermic needle in a dish over there which will make you feel lovely and sleepy while I actually get the bone out. Now, are we both ready? Let's go, Johnny. Don't let me down."

The lad gagged once and then was still and, following her actions from the lamp strapped to her head, Nancy fed the tweezers down the throat to the junction with the gullet. She had it! No, damn! It was slippery with the juices Johnny couldn't swallow. Now she *did* have it. Her look of triumph was conveyed to the lad, who was watching her hypnotically. Nancy beckoned Mrs Waddell, who was gloved and ready.

"Hold that. Don't let it go." Nancy gave the promised injection.

The hypodermic did its work and Johnny's eyes glazed over. This part could have been very painful for him, for Nancy had to tear the skin a little in twisting and removing the obstruction, quickly turning the boy to his side as blood spurted.

"Swallow now, Johnny," she said to him. "Don't go to sleep. Now spit for me." She held his head and a dish as Donald Wayne entered the room, his face one big question mark.

"We've just removed a nasty piece of jagged bone and Johnny's going to have a sore throat for a day or two," she said. "Would you like to take over?"

34

"No, you seem to be doing all right and you're sterile."

"Mrs Waddell, would you tell the parents it's all right now?"

Johnny was still spitting blood into a kidney dish but this became frothy and more pink as both doctors watched.

"Good lad! Dr Wayne, can Johnny take penicillin or would you prefer something else?"

"I'll look him up. Yes, he's OK on penicillin."

Nancy busied herself with another hypodermic, which she injected into the boy's buttock.

"Is it all right for me to make him up a gargle in our own dispensary? He's NH but the chemist won't be open till six. He's going to be sore when the injection wears off."

"Be a devil and do just that, Doctor."

Nancy wondered if her colleague was still laughing at her as she made up the pink antiseptic fluid for gargling, but he was still leaning against a desk and swinging one leg as she emerged from the small dispensary. She paused to wipe Johnny's blood-flecked mouth and sailed out to see the parents.

"He'll be sore for a few days, but bring him in on Wednesday to Dr Wayne's surgery for another injection of penicillin. Give him fluids only for a couple of days. He's sleeping at the moment, so if Daddy could carry him to the car?"

"Why can't we bring 'im to your surgery, Doctor? Arter all, it be you what done 'im."

Nancy realized these were incomers, like herself. They sounded as though they came from Devon.

"He's Dr Wayne's patient," she explained, feeling a surge of exultation nevertheless. "He'd have done just as I did had he been available. This is a gargle for Johnny. Every four hours. If he brings up a little blood, don't worry."

She was washing her hands and arms at the sink when she felt Donald

Wayne's presence beside her.

"Why didn't you rub my nose in it and tell them how they could change to get on your list? They're a family of six."

"Because I'm not a nasty opportunist, Doctor. I wouldn't expect you to take advantage of me in like circumstances and I live by the axiom do as you would be done by. Anything else?"

"Only thank you. I really am most grateful. I was in the gentlemen's cloakroom at the Dog and Duck where they failed to seek me when the telephone message came through. I came as quickly as I could."

"I'm simply glad it wasn't more serious. I had a tracheotomy setting all ready and would have dreaded meeting up with you if I'd had to resort to that."

"Lunch is ready, Doctors," Mrs Waddell's chest pouted more proudly than ever that she had been of such use to the new lady doctor. "Come on, now! No bones to swallow though it *is* roast pork."

"Shall we go in?" Donald Wayne asked a little awkwardly.

"Of course. I'm ravenous."

"Are you doing anything this afternoon?" he asked as they ate.

"Yes. I'm going out in the car and map-reading."

"I can help you with that. Let me see your map and I'll mark in the names of your patients."

"Thank you very much."

"Take your time. I'll be in for the rest of the day. We usually help ourselves from the fridge at suppertime on Sundays and have our meal al fresco. There's a film I want to watch on TV."

"I still have my patients' notes to study. Will you excuse me?"

"Certainly."

"By the way," she asked from the dining-room doorway, "did you shoot any ducks?"

"Three brace."

"You mean six?"

"No, I mean three brace. You must learn the terms. You may want to join a shoot one day."

"Oh, no. I couldn't kill anything. I'll bring you my map then. That would be a help."

"Anytime."

★ ★ ★

Nancy's first surgery on the Monday morning, her first official working day, brought her up against the realities of her new appointment. Dr Gray hadn't a large National Health practice, but when the new locum looked into the waiting-room she saw seven people sitting on chairs on her side, and about twenty-two waiting to see her colleague. She had been told to ping her desk bell twice for patients to enter, and this she did promptly at nine o'clock. A middle-aged woman eyed her very suspiciously and handed her a pink card with the number two on it.

"Where's my first customer?" Nancy asked lightly.

"Oh, Ned Phillips made off like a scalded cat when 'e saw you were a woman," the newcomer said. "We've never 'ad a lady doctor 'ere afore."

"Well, now you've got one for a while so you'll get used to it. We all get the same training, men and women. Now you are — ?"

"Amelia 'askins. I 'aven't been for three days, Doctor. It's getting chronic."

Nancy knew better than to ask 'Been where?'. The human race worried more about its bowels than any other of its bodily functions.

"I'll just look up your notes, Mrs Haskins. Ah! I see you are troubled by constipation. Have you followed Dr Gray's advice and eaten plenty of fibre for breakfast?"

"*That* awful stuff?" the woman complained. "I've allus 'ad my bacon and egg and my bacon and egg I intend 'aving. I think these newfangled notions are ridiculous. I never used not to be able to go. I think I've got a blockage."

"I hardly think so, Mrs Haskins. You couldn't enjoy bacon and egg with a blockage. If you don't like the special breakfast cereal, I'm sure, here in the country, you get plenty of green vegetables?"

"I don't like cabbage and that stuff. Just give me something to clear me out, Doctor."

"I can't do that, Mrs Haskins. You *must* eat the correct foods as well as those you like. Purging only makes the bowel limp, and then it stops working again. I'll give you a list, and three of the items you must take every day without fail. Also go for a good walk at least once a day."

"I'm allus on me feet — "

"That's not the same. Walking's the perfect exercise." Nancy was getting a little tired of her first patient. "If you haven't been relieved in two days, after following my instructions, let me know and I'll arrange for the District Nurse to give you an enema."

"An' I get no medicine?"

"You don't need any. Eat the correct foods and let nature take its course. Good day, Mrs Haskins."

"Well — !"

Ping! ping! went Nancy's bell.

Number Five came in, a post-shingles case in need of a tonic, then six and seven, an asthmatic and an arthritis sufferer, both women. Nancy peeped out to see if three and four had been overlooked, but only Dr Wayne's remaining patients regarded her curiously, one or two with knowing smirks on their faces.

The partners met over coffee.

"Well," Donald Wayne asked cheerfully enough, "how did it go?"

"I suspect you already know three of my flock fled away. Did anybody come to you from my side?"

"Young Ned Phillips tried to. He's having a course of injections in the buttock for acne. I told him you were the one to continue the treatment Dr Gray had ordered, and that you must have seen many men with their pants down over the past five or six years and not to be a young fool. He'll be back tomorrow."

"I haven't, actually," Nancy ruminated. "Seen all that many pants taken down, I mean." Her dimples played as she smiled up at her companion. "In hospital I was mainly on women's wards. I fancied taking up gynae, you see."

"And why didn't you?"

"That would mean telling you the story of my life and I don't think you want that, Doctor."

"No. That's a two-way thing. Better to keep a working partnership than get involved. I've had to put up with quite a few comments about you this morning as it is. 'You fancy 'aving a woman about the place then, Doctor? Pretty, isn't she? I bet she livens the place up.'"

"So they think I'm pretty?" Nancy

tossed her fair hair. "That makes up for losing a patient or two."

"I find most women thrive on superficial compliments but can't take criticism."

"And have you known many women? Apart from patients, that is?"

"That would involve telling the story of my life, Doctor, and I don't think you want that. Let's just say I'm not a monk."

Nancy heard her own words thrown back at her and swallowed her irritation. This very good-looking male, with his thatch of black hair and eyes like grey steel, was not prepared to be friendly, only professional when he had to be.

"Now I must make my visits," he said briskly. "Don't worry about your missing patients. I won't encourage them to cross the floor. After all, they are Dr Gray's responsibility, really."

Nancy lunched alone, eyeing the vacant place across from her resentfully. Was he trying to avoid her if he possibly could? She had decided to visit her chronics at their homes that afternoon, remembering Dr Gray's instructions to be prepared to listen sympathetically and carrying a docket of notes with her. Also she had had a telephone request from Mrs Wainwright, she of the possible peptic ulcer, to call on her if convenient at Hazel Tree Farm, where she was having a day in bed.

"Sorry to send for you, Doctor. But I 'ave been very queer."

"That's all right, Mrs Wainwright. I'll be in your vicinity anyway."

"'Scuse me, but you sound like a lady."

"I may not be a lady, but I am a woman, apparently to everyone's surprise. Don't worry. I have read up your case and will see what I can do to help. Don't eat any fats or rich foods."

"Ooh — I couldn't."

But, first, Nancy stopped the car at number three Ploughman's Cottages, on the edge of the village itself. The cottages were built of the silver stone

45

prevalent in the valley, a little dour but permanent-looking and all with their tiny walled areas of garden, shining with dahlias and chrysanthemums or evergreen shrubs. There was a fine cotoneaster, scarlet with berries at the moment.

In number three a fire glowed in the grate and in a comfortable armchair, her feet on a padded stool, sat the eighty-four-year-old Mrs Ivy Jacques, her clawlike hands and deformed feet, in old felt slippers, telling their own story.

"Hello, Mrs Jacques. I'm your doctor while Dr Gray is away."

"A lass? Thou'rt only a lass."

"I'm old enough. How are you today?"

"Oh, fine. I 'as me ups an' downs, like, but at my age what can you expect, eh? Hey! T'kettle's on the boil. Bring the tray out o't' kitchen an' we'll 'ave a cup o' tea, eh?"

Nancy was to find that all her visited patients plied her with refreshment.

She practically became awash with tea. With a cup in her hand she heard how the home-help came in every day to 'do' for her and make her dinner. Also she would have any prescriptions made up.

"So leave it there, love. Eh, but you're a bonny lass! I can't get over it. Done me good you 'ave."

Having assured herself that Mrs Jacques was helped to bed each evening by a neighbour, who also provided supper, Nancy washed up and refilled the kettle, leaving it on the hob, and prepared to go on to Rose Villa, to meet Mr James Watkin, a multiple sclerosis victim. He was fifty years old and seemed a bit shy of his visitor, but thawed out gradually to confide that he minded not being able to drive his car any more.

"I can look after myself, but the tremors come on unexpectedly. I've broken nearly all my tea-set. My wife's favourite. It's a good thing she's gone and doesn't know. I'm writing a book about my experiences."

"Oh?" Nancy looked interested.

"Yes. So long as I can write I may get something down which may help other sufferers. Provided I get published, that is."

Nancy stayed about half an hour, trying not to let the thought intrude that home visiting was extremely time-consuming. She next visited a chronic osteo-arthritis sufferer, with a very painful hip.

"I believe you are considering having a replacement operation, Mrs Pearce?" Nancy asked, while Mr Pearce, now retired, made the inevitable tea.

"Well, I'm a bit of a coward. I'm frightened, like."

"Nobody's going to force you, my dear, but it's usually a very successful operation, and then there's no pain in the hip at all. People often have both hips done. Think of that! You'd be able to walk again, with crutches and then sticks, maybe without any aids eventually. Why not see the specialist and at least have a talk with him? He would leave the decision to you. What do you think, Mr Pearce?"

"Well, it upsets me, like, when she cries in the night. It gets bad at night."

Eventually it was agreed that Nancy write the specialist at the nearest hospital and ask for an appointment.

"I'll say you're in great pain, Mrs Pearce, so you won't be kept waiting too long. Your heart's good, your blood pressure's fine, so I would say you're basically a healthy woman and could be helped. Now I must push off."

The last of the visits, before Nancy went off to see Mrs Wainwright, was the least pleasant, she discovered. It was to two sisters, living in a sort of ancient glory in a gloomy house which had known better days, with a large overgrown garden.

Miss Pansy Hulme was dark and gaunt and did not seem at all pleased when Nancy introduced herself. It was Miss Lily who was the patient; brain-damaged as a child of ten she had never grown up mentally since that time, though her body was large and thick and her ringleted hair greying at the temples.

"I've been thmacked," she announced, rubbing her buttock and looking coy. Her dress was lacy and too short, showing heavy fat-layered legs resembling an unhealthy baby. "I broke a thauther. Naughty Panthy hit me hard."

"Shut up, Lily! You hear me? This is the new doctor."

"Ooh! I like playing doctorth. I like thticking needleth in thingth."

"Will you be quiet? Go and swing."

The younger woman sulkily went out into the garden.

"Does Lily ever attend an institution?" Nancy asked.

"Why? Has anybody been complaining? I've looked after her all these years."

"I only thought she might respond to companions afflicted like herself. It must be very difficult for you to cope at times."

"I hope I know my duty, Doctor. Lily is the cross I have been asked to bear. I have borne it these forty years."

"But why must you? Society can help you and — and wants to. After all, you might not always be here. What about that?"

"I don't think about that. It's most disagreeable of you to bring it up."

"I'm sorry. I didn't mean to offend you. I simply thought you didn't look well."

"Well? I have always been well. What makes you say a thing like that? Have I complained?"

"No, but I can imagine coping with a fifteen-stone child must be very fatiguing. If you won't consider yourself then somebody must."

"I don't like to say this to a professional person, Doctor, but please mind your own business. Lily sometimes gets excited and has to be given sedatives. If you will leave a prescription that is all I require of you. After all, you won't be here always, either."

Nancy felt nettled by having her own words thrust back down her throat for the second time that day, and the oppressive atmosphere of the Grange made her long to get away. She wrote a prescription, said "good-bye" and went out into the tangled garden. A heavy swing was gyrating madly but there was no sign of Lily. Just as she was climbing into the car a half brick struck the bodywork, denting the panel. A cackling laugh came from the dense undergrowth. Her heart beating quickly Nancy started up the engine and accelerated out into the lane.

"That could have killed somebody," she thought as she drove away. "What a tragic case! I'd like to pass those two on to my partner if I only could! They give me the creeps."

# 3

THE sense of oppression did not leave Nancy until she arrived at Hazel Tree farm, and upon ringing the old-fashioned bell was greeted by a cheerful, middle-aged plump woman with the rosiest cheeks she had ever seen.

"You can't be Mrs Wainwright?"

"Yes I am. I know you're the doctor, but I didn't realize you would be so young. Come on in! I feel a fraud dragging you out 'ere."

"What happened to the day in bed?"

"Well, I got bored, and I felt better, so up I got. Any'ow, my William's down in five-acre field, with Sam, the lad we employ, an' who'd 'ave let you in, eh?"

Nancy managed to stop the kindly woman from putting the kettle on.

"I really couldn't," she said. "We'll

53

sit down and talk about you, shall we? How's the acidity?"

"Well, funny you should ask that, Doctor. It's gone. I enjoy my food; though I try to remember no fats. But what's bothering me is my stomach 'as dropped right down. That's what made me feel so queer this mornin', I was 'oldin' it up and it was squirmin' an' wrigglin'. I never 'ad nothin' like that 'appen to me before. But wouldn't you believe it? Now you're 'ere, like, me symptoms 'ave all disappeared, apart from the fact that I do know I'm 'eavier than I was. I never was a little un, but — "

Nancy was trying to consider the woman's tale of her symptoms and reason them out as a doctor. She had assessed her patient promptly as no malingerer, a busy farmer's wife could not afford to be. Yet she had felt unsettled enough, earlier, to put herself back to bed. She looked very well, so stifle the thought that she could be carrying a growth in her abdomen to account for the feeling of heaviness.

"I think I'd like you on the sofa, Mrs Wainwright, or up on your bed if anybody's likely to come in. I want your underclothes off. You can keep your dress on because we can hold it up."

"Oh, nobody'll come in yet. They've got to make the most of the daylight, the men 'ave."

First of all, Nancy used her eyes. The woman was overweight but not gross and her flesh was firm. Next she palpated the abdomen asking "Any pain or discomfort when I do that?"

"None, Doctor."

Nancy pressed, coming down lower into the swollen abdomen.

"Ah!" gasped Mrs Wainwright. "It's starting again, just like it did this mornin'. Squirmin' an' wrigglin'."

Nancy distinctly felt the movement, removed her hands and saw with her own eyes a distinct rolling under the skin before it subsided.

"There!" said Mrs Wainwright, her

brown eyes large with enquiry. "It's stopped. What *is* it, Doctor?"

Nancy was busy fixing her stethoscope, feeling strangely excited.

"I think I can answer your question in just one moment, Mrs Wainwright. I need to listen. Just lie still."

There it was in her ears, clear as a bell, the quick tum-tum, tum-tum of a foetal heart beat.

"Mrs Wainwright, I have news for you. You're going to have a baby."

The woman sat up, modestly covering her nakedness.

"I'm going to what, Doctor? A baby? Me? But me an' my William 'ad accepted the fact that I couldn't, or summat. What will folks say? Me at my age! Are you sure, Doctor?"

"Pretty convinced. The wriggling and squirming you complain of are baby's exercise periods, and I've heard his heart beating quite clearly. Or it could be a her. Would you mind?"

"Mind, Doctor? I'm that flummoxed I don't know what to think. Why did I 'ave this nasty acid stomach, then, an' sometimes I was sick."

"Well, when it's early days the uterus — that is the womb — is higher up and as it swells it presses on the stomach and can cause acute indigestion *and* sickness, mainly in the morning. Then after three months the uterus drops and the symptoms are relieved in most cases, though some people have acidity for almost the whole of pregnancy. But you look to me to be well on your way, seven months, perhaps, which is why you're feeling well in other ways. Could you be seven months? How long since you saw — ?"

"I never seen nothin' for more'n a year, Doctor. So 'ow could I?"

"It happens, Mrs Wainwright, and it's happened to you. Now aren't you going to give me a big, happy smile?"

The woman smiled a little tremulously. "Oh, Doctor, I allus wanted to 'ave a baby. Will an' I talked about it when nothin' 'appened an' 'e said 'Never mind, love. If it be God's will then

57

we've got each other.' What Will'll say I don't know."

"He's going to be thrilled to bits and concerned only for you. After all, we don't get a forty-three-year-old first-time mother every day of the week and we've got to act quickly. I need to phone the hospital and make an appointment for you to see the baby doctor, who'll book you in for the delivery."

"Oh! Can't I 'ave it at 'ome?"

"Not a chance! I wouldn't accept the responsibility. You're going to be a good girl and do as you're told, aren't you?"

"O'course, Doctor. A baby! Gosh! but I'm getting quite excited."

Nancy phoned up the nearest hospital with a maternity unit and spoke to the Consultant Obstetrician. He was as startled as she had been.

"I'd better see the dear tomorrow. She could drop it any time. I know these countrywomen. Get her to bring a specimen and I'll see her at eleven a.m.

precisely. I'll report back to you, Doctor — who did you say?"

"Devine."

"And are you? Ha! ha! Don't mind me, dear. You say you're Arthur Gray's locum? Well done! I'm having twins, so please excuse me. We're shouting a bit about it."

"Goodbye, sir, and thanks."

Nancy gave Mrs Wainwright her instructions and said she would send her a container for her sample.

"I see your husband coming," she said, packing her bag, "so I'll leave you to tell him your great news in your own way. He'll be able to take you to hospital tomorrow?"

"Oh, yes. This — " she patted her abdomen — "is what's important, now."

"You'd also better rally all your friends and get your layette ready for baby. What a lovely job! I do believe I envy you. Well, I must go. I have a surgery to attend. 'Bye, for now, Mrs Wainwright, and many

59

congratulations."

She saluted the husband, weathered to leather-brown and smoking a pipe, and went quickly back to Crag Lee, just in time to be given yet another cup of tea and a slice of Victoria-sponge cake.

"I need to talk to Dr Wayne, Mrs Waddell."

"Oh, he's started surgery. He sees children half an hour early twice a week, then carries on normally at five-thirty. You'll see him at dinner."

"That will have to do. I've had quite an afternoon one way and another."

★ ★ ★

There were more people at Nancy's surgery that evening, including the three who had fled at her earlier initiation, but still she was finished long before her colleague and decided to have a sherry before dinner at Mrs Waddell's urging.

A wind was rising and there was a soughing sound out of doors and the rush of leaves bowling along. The elements had always affected her and wind made her feel excited and yet sad at the same time, for really she had nothing to be excited about, like the prospect of a lover waiting to call on her or a great event to anticipate. This was a working job, and she could not see beyond the six months of her contract at present. She even allowed herself to remember Barry and the way she had had to fight clear of him and his embraces, like coming out of a rugby scrum. Barry was a very physical person; he had never listened when she had put on a Chopin record as a background to their activities, but had concentratedly chased her lips like a collector after a rare butterfly.

"I'll follow you," he had told her, when she had broken the news to him that they were not having a love affair so much as a wrestling match and that she had to go and get a better job. "You may sneer at the attraction of the sexes but it grows with time into something deeper. I'm not just letting you toss me aside. I'm very fond of you, Nancy, and I think your tragic loss has knocked you a bit off your rocker temporarily. I'm allowing for that, anyway."

At this moment in the empty room with the wind howling down the chimney, Nancy would have given a lot to see Barry coming through the doorway and throwing wide his arms to enfold her, squashing her flat, removing her breath and eventually leaving her limp and exhausted.

Mrs Waddell came in with a covered dish and proceeded to remove one set of cutlery from the dining-table.

"What — ?" asked Nancy.

"He said he wanted his dinner in his flat. I took it up."

"But didn't you tell him I wished to see him?"

"Yes, I did, Doctor. He said to tell you to give him a ring if it's important."

"*If it's important?*" Now Nancy

had all the excitement she needed in prospect. She was blazing with indignation and ready for a good row. "Where *is* this flat?" she demanded. "How do I get to it?"

"Well, Doctor, there's an outside staircase by the surgery. But I — What about your dinner?"

"Keep it hot, Mrs Waddell. I won't be long. You go on home."

She swept out of doors as she was. The wind was cool and tore wisps of hair over her face so that she could scarcely see in the dark to climb the stone staircase by the surgery wing, but she made it and felt about for a doorbell, finally hearing its shrill note resounding through the flat. The door opened to reveal a small hall almost entirely filled by a tall young man with his tie hanging loose and the top bottom of his shirt undone.

"Doctor Devine? To what do I owe this pleasure?" The grey eyes held no welcome, however. "Is the house on fire? Has Mrs Waddell broken a leg?

63

All the emergency services are listed on the pad."

"Mine isn't," she almost spat. "I want to know before we go any further. Are we partners in this practice or are we fighting a cold war because you resent a member of my sex invading your territory? I got the message all right from the start with you, so don't worry, I won't bother you more than I need. But when I say I want to see you it's about a matter I can't very well discuss over the phone. I don't care if you don't want to share the dinner table with me. You can have your meal up here every night if you prefer. Your company hasn't been scintillating up to now so I won't miss it. But to be fobbed off and told to ring you if my business was important was too much. I wouldn't have asked to see you for anything that wasn't important. You must have the biggest ego I've witnessed in any man, and I've met some big-heads in my time. Just who do you think you are? If Dr

Gray had asked to see you, you would have gone to him. Well, I am Dr Gray's *alter ego* while I'm here. I deserve the same courtesy you would show him."

All this while the young man, angry, now, had been advancing a step at a time, while Nancy had backed to keep out of reach. She felt space behind her and knew she had arrived in a bigger room. She decided to retreat no more, and looked around. The room was pleasantly furnished in a brown, tweedy way. There was a tweed-flecked fitted carpet and brown chairs and a deep sofa. On the sofa sat a woman, smiling in obvious amusement. She was a very pretty woman with cap-cut brown hair and eyes flecked with green. She was smoking a cigarette through a long holder.

"Don't mind me," she said in a low, musical voice. "I quite enjoy a good fight."

"Dr Devine," Donald Wayne introduced in a voice of ice, "Sister Temple."

How-do-you-dos were exchanged, with Sister Temple still smiling and Nancy feeling more of a fool by the moment. Her excitement and anger were diminishing now, frozen into immobility by the steel lances of those eyes still upon her.

"So if you would kindly leave, now, Dr Devine, I'll be glad to call and discuss whatever you are so eager to discuss in about an hour. Will it keep that long?"

"I — I — yes. I'm sorry. I don't know what to say. I obviously wasn't aware that you had company."

"I will tell you next time if you think I should," came straight out of Antarctica.

"No, of course not. I apologize most humbly. Sister Temple — ?" Nancy crept out into the small hall and made to open the door.

"Just a moment," came the chilling voice again. "You've become over-heated and are likely to take a chill." He seized his college scarf off a peg and wrapped it around her neck in a way which made her think he would like to choke her. "There! I'll switch the outside light on and see you later."

Only he could have made it sound like a threat, she thought miserably, as she crept back into the main house. She couldn't face dinner but had another sherry. What devil in her made her act Donald Wayne's fool? she wondered. Always he seemed to come out on top, justified by his actions and bright and shining. She had invaded his privacy and shrieked out her accusations and complaints like a harpy in front of a third party, a highly entertained third party at that.

"I'll bet she tells everybody and they laugh," Nancy brooded, drinking more sherry.

By the time she admitted Dr Wayne, prompt on the hour as he had promised, she felt befuddled and nervous. She ducked as he raised his hand to smooth his plentiful hair.

"I — I thought you were going to

hit me," she said with a hiccup.

"I never hit women, or, rather, I haven't up to now. Why haven't you eaten dinner?"

"How do you know I haven't eaten dinner?"

"Because your cutlery's still on the table."

"You must know how terrible I'm feeling? I couldn't eat. I'd have choked. I used to live such a blameless life and now I'm always having to apologize to you for some transgression or other. Why am I like this?"

"Because from the molehill that arose out of your being a woman, a fact I was not informed of, has grown this mountain of resentment in your mind that I am out to obstruct and make life difficult for you. Nothing could be further from the truth. I don't hate you, I don't love you, you just happen to be a colleague in a dress. I don't feel I should spend my time running after you now that you know the ropes. We go our own ways. If you wanted to see me this evening you had only to lift up the house-phone and say so. Now what was it all about?"

Nancy had picked up a cushion and was crying into it, however. She hadn't had a good cry for years and now it all seemed to be catching up with her. She found once started she didn't seem able to stop, though four glasses of sherry had certainly helped to unleash the floodgates.

"Please, *please* don't cry. Here!" He wrestled the cushion away from her and gave her his large handkerchief "I'm going to make you a sandwich and you'll eat it and then be sensible. I don't want to say anything rude about women's tears or you'd take it the wrong way again. But chaps don't cry."

"I — I don't, usually. I didn't even cry at my parents' funeral. I — I'll stop in a minute."

Sniffing, she eventually bit into the ham sandwich he brought her.

"If you've left Sister Temple I — I

suppose my news will keep till morning."

"Sister Temple has gone. We have all night to talk shop, though I do think you need a good sleep. I'm on call. Your turn tomorrow night. Now, what's your news."

"Well, I thought you ought to know that Dr Gray had made a wrong diagnosis. Easily done, and I could have made the same mistake myself some weeks ago. Mrs Wainwright of Hazel Tree Farm, was being treated for a query peptic ulcer because of her complaint of acidity. She's forty-three and sent for me today. I examined her and to her and my surprise she's about seven months pregnant. She's seeing Mr Mather tomorrow to be confirmed and booked in. I thought — hic! I'm sorry, it's all that sherry — if you're in correspondence with Dr Gray that he should know. I only hope with this being a first baby, and her practically menopausal, that all goes well and the child's OK. It's too late to abort. I was very thrilled and yet concerned about it, and the longer I waited to see you the more annoyed I became that I couldn't share my news with you."

"How did Bill Wainwright take it?"

"I don't know. I left her to tell him."

"I'll bet he swooned and right now is in the Dog and Duck, standing round after round. Like you, I hope and pray all will be well. But middle-aged women can produce fine kids. She'll be in good hands under Mather. He fancies himself as a bit of a fop but is very experienced and kind. Now, before you go to bed, anything else?"

"There *was* something — it seems to have slipped my mind."

"Think, while you have me."

"No, it's gone."

"Then I'll go, too. By the way, I'm sorry about your parents."

"Yes, well, we decided no swopping of life stories, didn't we? That just slipped out. Thanks for coming and — and goodnight."

"Goodnight. Have a glass of hot milk."

When he had gone she stood with her back to the door, after locking it, and remembered what else she had meant to tell him.

"I wanted to ask him what he knew about Pansy and Lily Hulme, and tell him about the dent in the car. Anyway, at least we did talk. He neither hates me nor loves me. I'm just a colleague in a dress. I must remember that. I wonder if he loves her? I hated her on sight, grinning like that. But then, I'm not a man and she was very pretty in a *femme fatale* way."

★ ★ ★

Mrs Waddell was in a gossiping mood next morning when Nancy finished her surgery, as usual, about an hour ahead of her colleague. She brought coffee for two into the study, where Nancy was studying the notes of General Nicholas Yates, who was one of Dr Gray's private patients, had survived two strokes and open heart surgery and had phoned for an appointment at eleven for a general examination and a supply of drugs which kept him alive.

"May I join you for coffee, Doctor? I have a moment," and Mrs Waddell put the tray down confident of her welcome.

"Certainly, Mrs Waddell. I'll have mine black but sweet today, if I may, please? What sort of man is General Yates? Is he the type to have another seizure because I'm a woman?"

Mrs Waddell laughed. "Oh! You are a one, Doctor. No, he's a very nice man. You've landed a lucky one, there, because he has a son who's a barrister and a daughter who's a doctor in Manchester. If he's not sympathetic towards lady doctors, who should be? Miss Madeleine will have told her dad about any injustices in the medical world."

"I'm glad about that. But it is a bit different when you're actually being examined by a woman young enough to be your daughter, I suppose. I'll wear my glasses and comb my hair right back."

"You wear glasses, Doctor?"

"I have a pair with plain glass in them. I got them when I was in medical school to make me appear more studious in the professors' eyes."

Another gurgling laugh from Mrs Waddell. "Is the coffee to your liking, Doctor? It's best Blue Mountain. Dr Wayne prefers it to others I've tried, and I do try to please him especially since — " She paused and Nancy looked up.

"Since when, Mrs Waddell?"

"You do know that he was engaged to be married not long ago? I don't know what happened but she upped and went and he — poor soul! — had to tell everybody the wedding was off. It must have been mortifying for him."

"Well, maybe he broke it off, too, Mrs Waddell. Who knows? If people aren't right for each other it's as well they find out before they marry."

"But he was miserable, Doctor. He worked hard and kept up a front but *I* could tell. A woman can, I think. Just lately he's been a bit brighter, cheered up a lot."

"Maybe he's found somebody else. When I barged up there last night there was a very pretty woman looking quite at home with him."

"Really? What was she like?"

"I shouldn't really be talking to you like this. It's very naughty of us. She had smooth, nicely cut brown hair and greeny-brown eyes."

"That sounds like Sister Temple."

"It *was* Sister Temple. He introduced us."

"Well! I wonder if they're getting together again? A young woman would have to go a long way to better a man like Dr Donald. Oh! I would be pleased for him if it was what he wanted. *She* can be a madam, like some hospital sisters are, and she treated me like a — a domestic. Once she called me 'Waddell', without the

'Mrs'. I was that mad. 'Waddell,' she said, 'clear away, now, we've finished. I can't stand the sight of dirty dishes.' I nearly said 'Clear them away yourself, then, milady,' but I didn't want to upset him. She only addressed me the once like that, because I think he might have had a word with her. So she was up there, eh? Oh! I'd have liked to be a fly on the wall, not that I allow any flies to sully my walls. I actually thought, Doctor, when you came, you might be good for him. That — that you'd take to each other with a bit of luck and a good push. But I expect you have a young man, a pretty little thing like you?"

"At the moment I'm steering clear of involvements. This job is enough without distractions, though I may have a man friend call in on me. He climbs mountains and things and we're not far from the Lake District, are we? He's not what you would call my young man. He's another doctor. That's all."

"But you're not a man-hater?"

"Not at all. Now I must go and find those glasses of mine. You'll see there's a clean sheet and blanket on the examination couch, Mrs Waddell? Thanks! You're a dear."

# 4

GRADUALLY Nancy was becoming assimilated into the life of Greendales and Crag Lee. Her surgeries produced Dr Gray's patients in increasing numbers as it was realized her sex had no effect upon her efficiency. In fact her more up-to-date approach was attractive to some people, especially younger women and mothers with children.

The weeks were passing almost imperceptibly and it was now autumn with a vengeance. Where the crag did not shelter, cold winds blew and robbed the trees of the last of their leaves; when the wind wasn't blowing it rained and there was early sleet at the end of November. Farmers forecast an early, white winter and were busy erecting 'nurseries' for any Christmas lambs which might decide to present themselves whatever the weather.

Nancy was making her monthly visits for the third time. She included a call on Mrs Wainwright, who was nursing a bundle of pink and white to her ample breast. The two women looked at each other and laughed.

"Well?" asked Nancy. "How's my lovely little namesake?"

The baby was to be christened Annette Georgina Wainwright, and looked like being blonde at the moment.

"Fine, as you see, Doctor. I still can't believe she's mine, some'ow. William looks at 'er an' says 'She's just like a piece of porcelain, the little darlin'.' Do you remember, Doctor, the day she came? First, I don't know I'm pregnant an' then I don't know I'm in labour. You must think me a proper fool," and Mrs Wainwright laughed happily again.

"I should just think I do remember that day. I'll never forget you, my dear, as long as I live. I got a message that you were feeling a little 'Queer', as I think you put it, and dashed over here to find I could actually see baby presenting. I was a bag of nerves and didn't know what to do for a moment."

"So you told me to 'old, rushed over to the phone, and I can remember the exact words you spoke. 'Dr Wayne,' you said, 'I want you at Hazel Tree Farm instanter. We're having a baby in the bed. No time to get the ambulance 'ere,' you said. An' you'd got Will boiling kettles an' pans an' I was surrounded by clean white sheets an' when Dr Wayne arrived you was 'olding my baby an' lookin' very pale. 'What is it?' he said, an' you answered 'I 'aven't 'ad time to look,' an' I said, 'I 'ave. It's a little girl,' an' then you was both busy for ages cleanin' up. Oh, my. I can laugh now."

"We had to let Mr Mather at the hospital know, and he said if all was well, the District Nurse should be able to keep an eye on you, along with me, and so you got your own way, after all, and had your baby at home. I do believe you arranged it all."

"I'm very 'appy, Doctor, an' very grateful to you an' Dr Wayne an' Nurse Wilde. All's gone so well it could 'ave been my eighth rather than my first. But 'oo's a lovely girlie, then? 'Oo's 'er Dad's little gem?"

"I must go," Nancy said. "Though I could look at you both all day."

"No time for a cuppa?"

"Not today, Mrs Wainwright. Too much to pack in."

She had already been to see the Barclay ménage, after George, the widowed father, had brought the small Debbie to surgery covered in blue bruises. Having asked how it had happened and been told Debbie had fallen down a long flight of stairs, while she was in the charge of 'that bloody girl', Nancy had studied George Barclay for any signs of guilt in his own demeanour. He had been very tender and loving, however, and Debbie obviously adored him. Having ascertained that bruising was the only trouble, Nancy decided to call in on George one day just to assure herself that all was well. She had already learned that George didn't work on Thursdays and so had dropped in, meeting his surprised, but pleased look of inquiry with a quick, "I was just passing, Mr Barclay, and thought I'd ask if Debbie's bruises are disappearing?"

"Come in, Doctor. How kind of you! Actually they've turned from greeny-yellow to purply-black, so she actually looks worse at the moment, but that's the way of bruises, isn't it? She's very pleased about it. She says, 'Daddy, look at my wounds.' Debbie! Where are you? The nice lady doctor has called to see you. And come downstairs carefully. She's playing with her shop," he explained. "We stocked it up this morning with hundreds and thousands, dolly-mixtures and jelly beans."

"You'll be bringing her to me next with a toothache," Nancy smiled, sitting in the comfortable chair he indicated. "Are you looking after Debbie yourself, today?"

"Yes. I gave the girl the day off."

"Your domestic situation must be a bit — well desperate."

"You can say that, Doctor. After my wife died her mother came to stay for awhile, but we got on each other's nerves after a while. Debbie was getting spoilt, and I wasn't having that. Then I got a housekeeper, but she was about forty and looking for marriage. I wasn't — not then, anyhow. So she eventually left. Since then I've employed a neighbour's daughter, who couldn't get a job because she'd failed all her O-levels, to come in and see to Debbie and make her meals. She loves children, so that works, but Betty is a bit inclined to read her teenage romance books and leave the child to her own devices at times. Debbie broke her arm and fell down the stairs and each time Betty was in charge. I know you can't watch a kid every moment, and that everybody has accidents, but Debbie's going to get bigger and need a mother. I should get married again, and at times I seriously think about it, but how am I ever going to meet suitable women as things are? I shouldn't be talking to you like this, Doctor. I'm sorry."

"Oh, yes, you should be, George. I may call you George? Getting things off your chest is good for you. You should be able to go along to the pub for a drink with the boys in the evenings. How about babysitters?"

"Well, I'm a bit isolated here, Doctor, and most of the folk are families who only see one another in the evenings. Young folk go to the disco in Carnforth. I really can't see any way out. I put Debbie to bed and sometimes I listen to records and the news on TV and turn in early myself. That's my life and I'm thirty-three."

"I can see it's difficult for you, George. If you could get a babysitter, occasionally, is there someone you'd like to see socially?"

"Well, I met a very nice young widow, once, at a country fair. She had a little boy a month older than Debbie. The children played together and we had a good, long chat about our predicaments. She found being a one-parent family difficult, too, from a social point of view. I'd like to see her again, if I could, if only to talk. I don't know her enough to anticipate anything else but she did say, as we parted, that we might meet up again one day."

"Well, George, I'll keep my eyes and ears open to see if I can help with this babysitting business. You need somebody mature who doesn't attend discos. OK? So there you are, Debbie! Eaten all your sweeties in your shop?"

"No-o. They're for my scales to sell to customers. I just sold Teddy five jelly-beans. Have you seen my wounds? Look!"

Nancy looked impressed and then said she must be going. She filed George's problems away to help with if she could. A thirty-three-year-old he-man needed a woman as well as a child. She was also settled in her mind that George did not ill-treat his little girl, that her accidents had been quite genuine and hurt him as much as the child.

Now she was left with her least popular call on the Hulme sisters. Last month she had left the car well away from the house but walked most nervously the distance to the house, on the qui vive for Miss Lily's playful but — possibly — deadly tricks. Lily was inside, however, on that occasion, dressing and undressing a doll and apparently engrossed with her play. Miss Pansy had complained of a headache and looked very tired. Nancy had been glad to write out the prescriptions the sisters required and make her escape. She had not yet mentioned her feelings about these patients to her colleague. She didn't want to appear either hysterical or neurotic after such a short acquaintance.

On this occasion, however, her walk

to the house was interrupted, and once again her heart quickened its beat.

"I'm hiding," came Miss Lily's voice. "Find me!"

"Oh, there you are!" Nancy said, as she saw a plump arm sticking out from behind a tree. "I've found you."

"Now you hide. Go on!"

"Oh, I can't just now, Lily. I must see your sister."

"Will you play afterwardth?"

"If I've time. Now be a good girl. Are you coming in?"

"No. I'll hide and wait for you. Don't forget. I'll be able to thee *you*."

Nancy couldn't conceal a shudder as Miss Pansy admitted her. Her professionalism overrode her own fears as she saw the older woman before her. In just one month Miss Pansy had shrunk and was the colour of parchment. Her eyes were sunken into her head and appealed and repulsed in the same glance.

"Miss Pansy, you don't look well. Have you — ?"

"My stomach's a bit upset, Doctor. Please don't fuss. I do get these upset stomachs from time to time. You can give me something for it, can't you?"

"I could if I knew the cause, Miss Hulme. I really should examine you. How about getting on the bed and letting me see you properly? Lily's waiting for me to play with her at hide-and-seek, so she won't bother us."

"Oh, Doctor, I really can't understand you. I wish you wouldn't fuss me. May I have the prescription, please? I didn't have this trouble with Dr Gray."

"I think you're ill, Miss Hulme. You may not have been ill when Dr Gray saw you last. It's my duty to — however, would you like Dr Wayne to take over from me? I'm quite willing that he should see you."

"Dr Wayne is a good-looking young man and Lily gets crushes on people. She had one on Dr Wayne, once, when Dr Gray was ill. She sat on his lap and it was all very embarrassing. Now, Doctor, the prescription, please.

I suppose I may have some Milk of Magnesia for my stomach?"

Nancy wrote, remembering a case she had seen in London of a woman who had deteriorated quickly and looked as Miss Pansy did now. That woman had been co-operative, however, and cancer had been diagnosed in her spleen, an organ removable and mainly unregretted by the human body. Yet how could one say, "Miss Hulme, I think you might have cancer of the spleen, or liver, or stomach and you're going to die unless you're seen to?" This was one to be discussed with her partner. She would see him today.

So concerned was she that she had forgotten Lily waiting outside until she heard the accusation, "You knew I wath waiting for you. You thaid — you know you thaid — "

"All right. Show yourself and then hide your face. Count to fifty and then come and find me."

Lily appeared from behind some heavy laurel and made a great show of putting her middle-aged head in her podgy arms. "One — two — " she began, as Nancy looked for somewhere fairly obvious to hide. She was slim and found a pine-tree more than adequate. Soon Lily was pounding about, saying "Where are you? I'm theeking."

After a minute she found her quarry.

"Got you!" and she pounced, holding Nancy against the tree.

"Clever old you! Now, let me go, I have to get back home."

"One more game! One more!"

"No, Lily. Let me go."

Lily pressed her weight and the tree pressed into Nancy's tender places.

"Lily! You're being naughty."

"I'm bigger than you."

"Yes. You are. You're hurting me."

"Thoftie! Thoftie!"

"You'll get smacked. Pansy coming."

Lily backed off to look and Nancy made an undignified scramble out of the garden and down the lane. She heard Lily chasing, but Lily had been forbidden to go past the gate, and miraculously this teaching had stuck in her mind.

Feeling weak, Nancy got into the car and drove off as though from the very mouth of hell.

"That's two of them I've got to discuss with him," she decided, as she headed for Crag Lee. "I'll have the honors tonight, I know I will."

★ ★ ★

There was no surgery that evening and Dr Wayne had taken most of his meals in the house since that scene shortly after her arrival at Crag Lee. She had always remembered his description of her as a 'colleague in a dress' and tried to remain businesslike and amicable, not forcing herself on him or introducing topics which might be controversial between them. She fancied, egged on by Mrs Waddell's more personal interest, that he was romantically attached again, and the appearance of a grey Mini Traveller in the drive usually heralded the explanation that he would be dining upstairs, if she should need him, or at the Quaker Inn in a nearby village — famous for its catering — where she could do the same. Occasionally on his days off duty he would drive off and not appear until after midnight. Somehow Nancy never really managed to fall deeply asleep until she heard him garaging his car and knew he was safely home again.

On this evening, however, she was really glad to see him. Though she had taken a warm bath since her afternoon's travels she still had a stabbing pain in her side. She caught her breath suddenly as she sat down on the chair he was holding for her.

"What's up?" he asked, sharply. "A horse kick you?"

She tried to smile, though it was a sickly effort.

"Feels like it," she said. "Actually I've been 'playing' with Lily Hume and, as she said, she's bigger than me."

"What did she do to you? I'd forgotten that you've inherited that baggage along with the gorgon of a keeper she's got."

"I meant to mention them just after I came here. Lily threw a brick at the car on my first visit, fortunately just below the passenger side window but making a dent in the door and cracking the paintwork a bit. I've kept the car down the lane, since, but today *I* came in for her attentions. I had to play hide-and-seek with her. When she found me she crushed me against a tree and I think I may have bruised a couple of ribs."

"Or cracked them. I must have a look at you, later."

"You?"

"Yes, me, Nancy." They had been on first-name terms for some weeks, now. It was he who had said it was silly to remain formal, living practically in the same house. "I'm your doctor, my girl, as you're mine, I want no false modesty from you."

"Very well, Don. But I don't think I've fractured anything. I can take deep breaths without agony. However, it's the elder sister, the gorgon, as you call her, who worried me today. She looked terribly jaundiced and aged and pain-racked. I suspect a carcinoma somewhere but one can't get near her. 'Stop fussing' is all she'll say, and nags for their usual prescriptions. What do I do about her? She should go and see a specialist, but there's that great baby sister of hers running loose."

"There's one person who can control Lily, if anybody can. It's old Mrs Jenkins, who keeps the village shop. She used to be Lily's nursemaid when she was first taken ill, and stayed on as Nanny. Lily still calls her that. She loves her in her own way. I'm sure Mrs Jenkins would move into the Grange for a day or two while Miss Pansy visited hospital. Her daughter practically has sole charge of the shop, nowadays. To get Miss Pansy to move we must tell a few white lies. Dr

Gray is her gospel. You have talked on the telephone to Dr Gray and he asks that she see a specialist without delay for Lily's sake. If so be your worst fears are confirmed, then Lily must be put away, as should have happened long ago. Apparently Miss Pansy promised their mother on her deathbed that she would always look after Lily. Ah, me! Parents have a lot to answer for in these cases! Would you like me to talk to Miss Pansy on the phone? Arrange things if I can?"

"Would you? I'm just a fussy incomer after all."

It was all arranged within the next half-hour by phone. Mrs Jenkins would be glad to live in with Lily while Pansy was being examined in hospital. Pansy had reluctantly agreed, though she had to add that she thought it a bit high-handed of that lady doctor to telephone Dr Gray on her account. Still it was nice of Dr Gray to concern himself about her welfare, though gentleman that he was, she could quite understand it.

"So," Don Wayne said with a wry smile, "we ought both to go to church on Sunday and ask to be forgiven. Make a note to confide our little plot to the old man on his return, will you? Miss Pansy, if all should be well with her, will be sure to thank him for his interest and advice. Now come on into surgery and I'll have a look at you."

She tried not to be embarrassed as the strong, trained hands investigated her rib-cage, causing her to grimace but not to shout, then press on the sore spot while he listened to her breathing. His interest was all in his ears and an alien thought struck her that he really was a very handsome man, with dark hair trying to curl around his ears and long lashes shading keen steel-grey eyes, so that she couldn't imagine how Sister Temple could even consider letting him go out of her life.

"I was saying," came the voice into her thoughts, so that she realized he had removed his stethoscope from his ears and was regarding her, "that there's not much of you, but what there is does seem to be fairly sound. If you develop a cough or begin to feel rough report back to me. OK?"

"Yes, I will. Thank you."

As she dressed he kept on talking. "Watch out for Lily. I should have thought and given you a few tips. She likes comic-strip books, and if you remember to take a few along she'll probably disappear like a shot. Also she loves kiddie sweets, her taste in such things never having matured since her illness. You're her friend for life with a bag of liquorice allsorts in your hand, or jelly-babies."

"I'll remember."

"Ah! There you are. Nancy, I've just had the most awful thought. How long have you been here?"

"Nine weeks."

"And what social life have you had in that time?"

"We-ll, I've been to the Hall for

dinner, once; mainly to be looked over, I believe. I found it something of an ordeal, especially when the conversation got round to hunting and I revealed I had never even ridden a rocking-horse. I had a very pleasant evening at the General's, while his daughter was visiting, but, unfortunately, I was called out during dinner and couldn't get back. I think that's about all."

"Two occasions in nine weeks? You've sat here night after night on your own watching the wretched TV? A pretty young woman like you?"

"Oh, come on, Don! I'm not grumbling. I came here to work and I'm very good at entertaining myself. I take long walks, I gave the Rector tea one day when he called and we had a most enjoyable theological argument, and a couple of times I've been to the Rectory for a chat with Mrs Soames. I also read a lot."

"I could kick myself for my neglect. I should have taken you around and introduced you to people. I didn't think."

"Oh, look, Don, because I'm your colleague you are not to consider yourself my keeper. You have your own life to lead and I don't want you to think you have to entertain me. I enjoy our chats over meals. After all, you were really expecting a male locum, and after telling him what was what and maybe standing him a drink at the Dog and Duck you'd have left him to get on with doing his own thing, as I must. People who have to work together don't necessarily want to play together. Now you're not to worry about me. When term ends I'll have my sister here for a month. Life's never dull with Candy around, and if there's any life here she'll find it."

"So you have a sister?"

"Candida is reading Modern Languages at Oxford. She's very pretty."

"Oh?" The grey eyes lit with amused interest. "And what does that make you? The ugly sister? *I* think *you're* very pretty. I always have, even when you were angry with me and throwing insults around."

Nancy had flushed a little uncertainly. "Well, thanks, kind sir."

"I would like us to have at least one date together, if you can bear it. On Saturday we're both free. Dr Myers, in Carnforth, is covering the district. I have two tickets for an amateur performance of *The Gondoliers* in Kendal. I would suggest we have dinner first and see the show. The company is quite good as a rule if you like Gilbert and Sullivan. Would you — ?"

"Well, you're sure you wouldn't prefer to take someone else? I mean — with two tickets you must have bought them with somebody in mind — ?"

"No. I always buy two. It's for charity. Some years I can't go and give the tickets away. This time I'm free and so are you. Of course if you don't want to go I'll understand and not be offended. Amateur operetta isn't everybody's cup of tea."

"I think it sounds like fun. I was once in an amateur pantomime and that gave me a lot of pleasure. The audience seemed to like it, too. I'll go with you, Don, and thanks for asking me."

"Right! Be ready on Saturday at six. We'll eat at seven so don't have too much lunch and none of Mrs Waddell's high tea. Now I must go and get my beauty sleep as I'm on call, I believe? I've enjoyed our chat this evening, Nancy, and time has flown. Let me know if there's any development with the ribs, now, and if so we'll get you X-rayed. Can't have Doctor developing a rib-fracture pneumonia. Goodnight! I'll see myself out. Remember to lock up."

She felt quite cheered up when he had gone and looked at herself in a mirror to see what he thought was very pretty. Her oval face was flushed, her nose snub, whereas Candy's was short and straight, and her hair shone and was a little unruly from last night's shampooing.

She went to bed, felt her sore places and decided she mustn't develop anything as serious as a rib-fracture pneumonia to spoil her plans for the weekend.

She even awoke feeling happy and sailed through her work all day.

That evening the Mini Traveller was again parked in the drive and Don announced he would be dining out.

"Of course," she told him. "I'm going to write twenty letters. I've been most neglectful of all my friends."

She wondered if he would have taken Sister Temple to see *The Gondoliers* had she been free on the night.

# 5

NANCY considered her visit to the Rosery, a pretty little cottage on the edge of the village, most fortuitous in all ways. She was surprised that here she had two more spinster sisters living together, though in this case most amicably. Don Wayne had told her there were many spinsters in the area, some living in quite big houses, the reason being that parents had died, sons fled home for the cities and the girls left behind to live out their lives in the family homes. The Misses Grace and Pauline Penn, however, had actually left their home in a Yorkshire city to buy the Rosery and retire to Greendales, a district they much admired. Both had been schoolteachers, had inherited some money from an only brother and decided to enjoy their lives before they became too decrepit to do so. They were a youthful-looking sixty-one and fifty-nine respectively, with blue-rinsed hair and rosy cheeks. Miss Grace had a Colles' fracture, and was finding she couldn't sleep for the pain. Being private patients of Dr Gray, Nancy had volunteered to call and try to find out the reason for the pain and help if she could. She found both sisters waiting to greet her.

"How nice to see a lady doctor!" said Miss Grace.

"Yes. How very nice!" agreed her sister.

"Good of you to come," said Miss Grace. "Pauline could have driven me to surgery, but it's so painful getting into clothes."

"Yes, she finds dressing painful," Miss Pauline nodded. "I'll just put the kettle on. We don't get many callers. We're not natives, you see, and it's a very closed community."

"Very close. They keep themselves to themselves." It was Miss Grace's turn to act as echo on this occasion. "We tried to see if we could help at the school in anyway, with dinners or as playground supervisors, but Miss Pennyweight is a bit jealous of her authority, I suspect, and may have thought we were after her job. We have always been used to being busy bees, you see, and we sometimes don't have enough to do."

"Not nearly enough," Pauline shook her head vigorously. "Grace tripped and fell and broke her wrist just looking for jobs to do in the garden. But it's not the right time and we had it all tidy by the end of September."

"That's it. September. Only one apple tree to harvest but it was loaded, and we'll have apples well after Christmas. That was the last job, picking apples."

"Lovely apples, pale green cookers. What do you have in your tea, Doctor?"

"Just a little milk, please."

Nancy had been poking and probing

inside the plaster holding the fractured wrist. She managed to get a file inside and worked for a few minutes.

"I think that was a bit rough, Miss Penn, and there's a little too much play in the plaster. I'm going to force as much wadding down as I can to pack it, which should make it easier to bear, if you keep it in your sling as much as possible. Have you any painkillers? Well, I'll leave you a few more and you may take two every four hours, if necessary. Of course any fracture aches. You must expect that, but if it becomes unbearable then let me know and you must go and see the specialist again, maybe have a replastering."

"Oh, that feels much better, Doctor. I hope I haven't been wasting your time?"

"That would be awful of us," Miss Pauline grimaced. "Have a bit of Yorkshire parkin, Doctor."

"My time hasn't been wasted, especially if you're a little easier, Miss Penn."

"Anyway, it's nice to see a new face."

"Such a bonny new face."

"We don't have many visitors."

"No, not many."

"Not that we're grumbling. You can have too much of a good thing, people never off your doorstep. We wouldn't want that."

"I wonder," Nancy broke into the duet, "if you could do me a favour and help another human being?"

"How could *we* help, Doctor? We've offered our services where we could and been — I hate to say it — snubbed. You don't like to ask for that sort of thing."

"No, once bitten twice shy."

Nancy decided to tell the sisters the story of George Barclay and his motherless child. She told it in all its frustrating detail and emphasized what a nice fellow George was and how lovable his little girl, also how necessary it was he should be able to get out in the evenings sometimes.

"Oh! the poor young man. You mean you would want us to babysit, Doctor?"

"George would pay."

"Oh, no, he wouldn't. We couldn't let him. An act of Christian charity?"

"We could take our crochet work with us and put the little girl to bed if he liked. I'm used to children. My job was to look after the infants at my old school. At that age they were so nervous the first few days, one had to do simply everything for them."

"I took over where Pauline left off," said Miss Grace. "Mine were the sixes and sevens. We both love children."

"So you're saying you'll do it?" Nancy asked, not quite believing her luck.

"Of course we will. Yorkshire folk may be regarded as rough by some, but we're a soft-hearted lot."

"You may be kept up rather late — "

"So what? Who's to say we're to get up at any set time?"

"The wonderful thing is you've got

your transport— your own car — I suppose one of George's problems has been that he couldn't leave the house to take any babysitters home, even if they existed."

"They exist now," said Miss Grace, "if he takes to us. How do we let him know we're willing?"

"I'll phone him this evening," Nancy said, "and give him your number. He'll probably ask you to tea on one of his free days and you can discuss the matter and see little Debbie. She's a charming child and he adores her. Well, the parkin was delicious, ladies, but I must go now. Our housekeeper will scold me for not wanting any tea. Still comfortable, Miss Penn?"

"Yes, Doctor. You've done me — both of us — a lot of good. Bless you, love."

"I'll call in whenever I'm passing this way," Nancy promised, "though I might not be able to stay so long. Goodbye, for now."

She sang at the wheel of the old

doctor's car as she returned to Crag Lee. She'd phone George when she was sure he'd be home, take evening surgery and then it was a free weekend and her date with Don. He might well be somebody else's fiancé, but she was looking forward to it as though she had been starved of such things for a very long time.

* * *

Wondering how to dress for her unexpected evening's entertainment, Nancy decided she had been booted and mackintoshed for far too long and that to dress up a little would do her own morale some good. She had washed her hair in the morning and blown it dry so that it was fluffy, like a child's. A little conditioner brushed in brought it under control and it curled under her neck and round her heart-shaped face, apart from one wayward strip which always curled outwards, no matter what she did to dissuade it.

The day had been cold and bright and evening threatened frost, so she examined her limited wardrobe of clothes and decided on an amber-velvet dress with a swathed corsage and flared skirt. With velvet there can be only one jewel, the pearl, and Nancy had inherited her mother's single-strand pearl necklace and matching studs for her ears. Enough was enough and she was pleased with her appearance. Her watch had been a twenty-first birthday present and she only wore it on special occasions as it was too small to use in her doctoring. She approved her appearance and was busily applying a little golden-brown eye shadow above her chocolate-drop eyes when the internal phone rang.

"Ready?" asked Don Wayne. "I ordered dinner especially early. I hope you're famished?"

"I am. Mrs Waddell called it a lot of nonsense when I only had a spoonful of cottage pie at lunch time and no ice-cream. I'm ready. I'll just get my coat and gloves."

She let herself out of the house and locked up, partly fastened her brown needlecord cord under the light perpetually burning over the front door and heard Don's voice from near at hand.

"Dr Devine, you look a million!"

"Well, thank you, sir," she said. "I don't know how much one dressed for these occasions but I see you're in DJ."

He handed her into his car and down the lanes they went, the headlights picking out the skeletal arms of the bare trees until they reached that switchback she had remarked on her journey to Greendales in the taxi. Happily she squealed over each bump and Don laughed good-naturedly.

"I've long got used to that," he said, as the road smoothed out, "But I always like to hear somebody enjoying it. I have two small nephews who would ride it all day if they were allowed to."

"So you're an uncle?"

"Oh, yes. Four times over. I'm the youngest of my family and my two brothers and a sister are married. I'm sorry!" he smiled ruefully into the driving mirror. "I think we once vowed no confidences about our private lives, didn't we?"

"I think that was in our hackles-raised period and should be forgotten. We were both a bit touchy at first. Do you see much of your family?"

"Not a lot. I have a brother, Nick, the father of the two boys, who likes to shoot. He comes when he can and we bag a brace of duck. My other brother, Ben, is in Canada — we're all in medicine, by the way — and our sister, Sally, is married to a pathologist and lives in Surrey. She has twin girls."

"You must have had a wonderful childhood. I regretted not having brothers. I was always in charge of Candida, and she was too young to be a pal. However, families come in all shapes and sizes. It's a dark night, isn't it?"

"Yes. There's the rags of the old moon rise at about three-thirty a.m. I saw it last night when I was called out."

"Oh! I didn't know you'd had a call. Was it necessary?"

"My old Mrs Widdup died. She was ninety-four. She left us wept over by eighteen members of her family; children in their seventies, grandchildren, great-grandchildren and a great-great grandchild who slept through the event. She was a dear old character who made me mint humbugs every Christmas."

"You're going to be tired tonight."

"You can drive us home if I am. Now here's our restaurant. We have about an hour and I took the liberty of ordering so that all would be ready. The owner's wife is French and she is cooking the meal specially. Come on! Out you come."

Nancy had rarely tasted such

wonderful food. They were alone in the vast, warm dining-room in a corner by the fireplace, as normally the restaurant didn't open until eight. Don was obviously well known and his custom appreciated. First, there was a delicious pâté and fingers of hot buttered toast; this was followed by veal *Courvoisier*; the fillets of meat had been marinated in old brandy and were then fried in a batter of egg and breadcrumbs and served with button mushrooms, tulip-cup tomatoes and a bubbling brown cheese sauce poured over the whole.

"Gosh!" Nancy exclaimed at one point. "I'd like the recipe for this."

"Madame will always share her secrets, but don't you think half the pleasure is not having to get all hot and bothered in the kitchen? Now, drink up your wine."

"I soon get tiddly. Not too much, please, Don."

The sweet was another *Provençale* speciality of Madame's. It was a *compôte* of fruits in a choux pastry case, and was smothered in Benedictine.

"Where did I put all that?" Nancy asked, patting her middle.

"Actually, you haven't eaten much in bulk. Compare what you've had with English roast beef, Yorkshire pudding, two vegetables and rich gravy. Delicious, I know, but we do pile our plates as a rule and rise from the table wanting to go and lie down. Now, we must go. The evening is still young."

Nancy remembered to seek out Madame Williamson and thank her, and back in the warm car and speeding towards Kendal on the motorway, the brandy, wine and Benedictine had a cumulative effect on her, she leaned against Don and drowsed.

She came to herself in a brightly lit hall, where there was a loud buzz of conversation and Don showing her to a seat in the third row from the stage, and obviously acquainted with quite a few people.

"My colleague, Dr Devine. Mrs Nash. She's the producer of the show."

"How do you do. What a lot of work you must have put in!"

"Well, let's hope it goes well, Doctor. The dress rehearsal was a disaster."

"They do say it all comes right on the night."

"We must hope so."

Don produced a box of chocolates and laid them on her lap.

"Well, thank you!" Nancy was overcome. "You must have first pick — I insist — I like absolutely everything."

The show began rather nervously and self-consciously as the house lights were dowsed, and then the sheer melodiousness of the unforgettable score settled everyone down and the audience were more than ready to applaud every solo and chorus.

By 'Take a Pair of Sparkling Eyes — ', the chocolates were finished and reaching hands had somehow become entwined. Nancy was aware of pleasurable tingles as Don squeezed in time to the music.

"He's forgotten it's me," she told herself. "He's going to apologize any minute."

But he didn't. The lights went up for the second interval and he sighed and let go her hand without other comment then, "Enjoying it?"

"More than I can say. The first tenor has a very good voice, hasn't he?"

"Well, hello!" came challengingly. "I've been sitting over there and thought you were never going to notice me."

"Myra!" Don was obviously surprised. "You know Dr Devine?"

"Of course. Didn't I hear you having that lovely row when she first arrived? When did you stop tearing strips off him and start holding hands, instead?" came maliciously but trying to sound teasing. "I enjoyed you in the first role so much better, Dr Devine."

Nancy was embarrassed equally for

Don as herself and decided to ignore the attack.

"Are you enjoying the show, Sister Temple?"

"As much as one can enjoy these amateur dos. Of course charity benefits, doesn't it? One has to support charity."

"I think the curtain's going up, Myra. Better get back to your seat. Nice to have seen you," Don said mildly.

"*Au revoir*, then."

"*Au revoir*."

Nancy was now aware of a change in the atmosphere around her, and divided her time between watching the stage and covertly glancing at the figure across the aisle, equally intent upon watching her.

"Good for you!" came in her ear.

"Pardon?"

"I said good for you! You handled Myra very well."

"I don't want to come between a man and his — er — friends. Does she mind your bringing me here?"

"I hope so."

"Are you using me to make her jealous?"

"Certainly not. I didn't know she'd be in the audience. I brought you here for our mutual pleasure, and so far I had dared to hope it was pleasurable. Shall we hold hands again?"

"You *are* trying to annoy her, aren't you? Have you had a quarrel, or something?"

"We are always having quarrels or something. Don't let that bother you. Tonight is *our* night."

He seized her hand, refused to release it when she tugged and they glared at each other throughout the finale of the show.

Sister Temple left the hall rather ostentatiously just before the performance ended, her escort darting after her somewhat apologetically.

"Now there's no need for the charade," Nancy said quietly.

"Sorry! It wasn't a charade with me."

"But everybody knows — even *I*

know — that Sister Temple and you were engaged to be married. You're still seeing each other so one presumes you remain interested."

"Is that what one presumes? Come on! Let's get home. The glass coach has changed back into a pumpkin."

"I'm sorry if I rubbed a raw patch," Nancy said uncomfortably as they speeded along the motorway. "I shouldn't have mentioned your engagement when I only heard of it in gossip."

"Have *you* endured a broken engagement?"

"No. I — er — we never got as far as getting engaged. I thought I was fond of — of Barry, but I've started forgetting what it felt like to be with him."

"Maybe you're just forgetting what masculine attention feels like. You've lived like a nun for nine whole weeks."

"You brought me out, tonight, to make up for what you imagined I was missing, didn't you, Don? Hence the hand-holding and the chocolates and the compliments? If it damages your relationship with your true friends, however, I'm sorry I accepted your invitation. I've enjoyed myself so much but Sister Temple may hate me and take things out on you."

"I'll have to risk that. Myra doesn't keep me on a leash. I don't have to ask her if I may go out and play. She knows that. Nearly home, now. You must be tired."

"Not so tired as you, who had a disturbed night. I've just remembered I was supposed to drive home."

He watched as she unlocked the door of Crag Lee.

"Don't let's part like this," he requested, "with a quiet sense of outrage between us. Other people shouldn't be allowed to interfere."

"No sense of outrage," Nancy assured him. "What do you mean? I'm very grateful."

"That won't do," said Don. "I haven't been out with a maiden aunt."

He pulled her to him suddenly and his lips descended upon hers. At first she struggled and then she was lost in the experience itself. Whatever reason he had for kissing her it was enjoyable in its own right. She swayed slightly on her feet as he released her then she managed to say quite steadily, "Goodnight, Don. It really has been — most pleasant," and was closing the door behind her only to lean against it and think, 'Whatever reason he had for doing that it certainly did me good. He's attractive. He's nice. She doesn't deserve him.'

# 6

THE colleagues resumed their old ways as though that night had never been. Nancy did think about it on occasion, especially the final moments of their goodnight kiss, and what had preceded them, but Don looked so back-to-normal sitting across the lunch-table from her discussing a morning he had had to spend in a coroner's court, that she quickly decided he had merely intended to give her a really diverting evening, and had put his heart and soul into doing so. There was to be nothing significant read into the hand-holding and the kiss. They were mature adults, not raw teenagers, and had behaved normally for people of their ages.

Sister Temple's car still appeared in the drive quite regularly, and equally regularly Don went off in the evenings in his, when Nancy was 'on call' and officially in charge of the practice.

She was really quite pleased with her progress as locum to Dr Gray. George Barclay had phoned her up delighted after a visit from the Misses Penn, and was so grateful at the idea of being relieved of his parental duties for a couple of evenings a week.

"Debbie just loved those two dear ladies on sight," he said. "They have a great understanding of children. I don't know how to thank you, Doctor."

"Then don't, George. I'm simply glad the opportunity arose whereby I could bring you all together. The Misses Penn were so eager to be wanted by somebody, and now can feel a part of the community. I hope all works out well."

It was a less pleasant task seeing Miss Pansy Hulme again, who was now confined to hospital in a nearby town. She had an inoperable malignant tumour and had insisted on being told the facts. She had not collapsed into tears or appeared to panic, but when Nancy called to see her she felt as though Miss Pansy had been waiting for her.

"Well, Doctor, why don't you say 'I told you so'? You suspected this, didn't you?"

"One can never be sure, Miss Hulme. I thought you looked so poorly I was concerned for you."

"They can't operate, did you know?"

"Yes, I was told. But I believe you're having extensive chemotherapy. That works with some people."

"It makes me sick. I know I'm going to die, Doctor."

"Oh, come!"

"Don't 'oh come' me as though I was a child. I'm going to die and there's Lily to think about. That's what's bothering me."

"Lily's fine with Mrs Jenkins. I took her some comics and some sweets and she was very good. She asked about you and I said I was coming to see you. She sent her love."

"Did she ask when I was coming home?"

"Yes, she did." Nancy bit her lip. "I told her I would find out."

"When I die, Lily will have to be told."

"In that eventuality do you want me to tell her, or shall Mrs Jenkins do it?"

How can anybody discuss their own death so dispassionately? Nancy was thinking. It's weird. It's frightening.

"I don't quite know what Lily will do when she's told, without me there to control her. Our mother died just after Lily's illness and she nearly went mad with grief. Do remember, Doctor, that Lily is a normal ten-year-old who simply stopped growing up mentally. She has a ten-year-old's feelings in that huge, healthy body of hers. She loves old Nanny Jenkins but *I* disciplined her. It may be very difficult for a while controlling her when she is upset."

"I don't want you lying here worrying about Lily, Miss Hulme. I'll visit her

127

as often as I can and talk to her as a ten-year-old about how things and people do die. I'll spare her as much time as I can."

"Thank you. Now I'm in pain. Would you tell the nurse, please?"

"I will on my way out. Good afternoon, Miss Hulme."

"And the sixty-four thousand dollar question is — " Nancy ruminated as she walked down the hospital's long corridors — "what's going to happen to Lily Hulme when her sister does die? Mrs Jenkins is old and can't stay in charge much longer or I'll have another death on my hands. I'll talk to Don about it."

A doctor's life was not always a happy one, Nancy was discovering. One tried not to get personally involved in patients' problems, but how many doctors had a Lily Hulme or a George Barclay on their books?

Winter was approaching fast. On her calls Nancy saw farmers erecting pens near their farmhouses for their pregnant ewes. The winds could blow piercingly in that corner of England's green and pleasant land and they seemed to come off the high peaks of lakeland across the bay, stinging exposed cheeks to flame and chapping ungloved hands. One day the snow arrived and it lay, throwing silver reflections on the ceilings of houses and muffling all sounds without. The young doctors still had to go out to patients unable to tackle the elements, especially the old and arthritic, and Mrs Waddell pointedly laid out an assortment of Wellington boots for these excursions.

"I will not have you getting wet feet," she told her charges, "or snow melting on my good carpets. Now be off with you and there'll be hot soup for starters when you return."

"Have you realized," Don said as they shared the luncheon table that day, "it's only a fortnight to Christmas?"

"I know. I haven't even bought my cards yet, let alone presents."

"Ditto. You have Tuesday off for

shopping and I'll go on Wednesday. We'll take combined surgeries those days and have Mrs Macphie in to take notes." Mrs Macphie was an ex-shorthand typist who came in once or twice a week to keep the practice's books in order and send out any accounts for the doctors' services. "That's the way Dr Gray and I worked it when we wanted a bit of time off. Agreed?"

"Agreed. Candy will be coming any day, unless she has decided to spend Christmas more excitingly with some of her university friends."

"Would she do that to you? Leave you alone at Christmas, I mean?"

"Like a shot. You're only young once, Don, and Greendales isn't exactly the hub of the universe when you're twenty-one."

"Some people like it. The waits come round and we all go to church, even if it's only once a year. Also the young folk are home from boarding-school or university and there's a hunt on Boxing

Day, with a ball afterwards at the Hall. It's real Christmas-card stuff, and I think much better than the artificial business in the towns."

"Do you hunt?"

"No. But I wasn't country bred and staying on a horse isn't easy for me. I'd rather stand and watch the experts."

"I heard from Barry — you know, the fellow I didn't get engaged to? and he asks if he may come and spend a few days at Christmas. I suppose I can get him in at the Dog and Duck?"

"Or he could stay with me. I have two bedrooms. No, no! What am I thinking of? The Dog and Duck would be better."

"But why?"

"Well — " Don went pink — "I don't want to know what time he comes in or goes out, do I? I'd feel I was spying on you."

"Don, I've told you, it isn't that sort of a relationship. We're friends, that's all."

"Well, if you're never given the

opportunity you'll always remain friends, won't you? Stop behaving as though you're on the shelf, Nancy."

"It's a different matter being on the shelf to leaping into the wrong man's arms."

"What's wrong with this Barry?"

"Nothing. He's quite good-looking, has lots of fairish hair. He plays rugby and likes fell-walking. I think that's why he wants to come here, not because of me. Incidentally, he has no family so hasn't anybody to consider at Christmas but himself. Anyway; I've told him he'll be welcome if he cares to come."

"I'm expecting a Christmas baby. Otherwise I'd have gone home for a couple of days. The mum's going into hospital but she wants me there. Anyhow, Mrs Waddell leaves plenty of food and I expect you can cook?"

"I'll do my best."

"I'll clear off as much as I can while your — er — friend's here."

"I'll shake you in a minute! This is your home, more than mine, and I won't have you clearing off as though you're in the way. You can be very aggravating at times, Don."

"I know. Everybody's always telling me so. Now to work."

"Me, too. Gosh! look at the time! and it gets dark so early nowadays."

★ ★ ★

Candida Devine was having the time of her young life holding court in a train. Ever since she changed into the slow train at Preston, first class, of course, for which she expected to be reimbursed by her older, working sister, seeing that she was going to brighten up Nancy's life by her visit, she had sat looking demure in a bright blue coat with a fur collar, her blue eyes peeping out from under upswept, perpetually questioning brows and her naturally fair hair gleaming under the carriage lights, and had known herself to be the cynosure of two pairs of decidedly interested masculine eyes. After the ticket collector had assured her that she must detrain at Carnforth for Greendales, the taller and handsomer of the two young men had approached.

"Excuse me, Miss — "

"Yes?" The blue glance struck the hazel eyes like two icicles, just to let him know she wasn't easily picked up, though her heart had quickened a little at his interest.

"I — I just happened to hear you're going to Greendales. I thought I knew everybody who lived there. I'm Jeremy Huntley from the Hall, post-gradding at Queen's, Oxford, and on my way home for the vac. Are you being met?"

"You couldn't know me, Mr Huntley. My sister is acting as locum to your Dr Gray and this is my first visit. I'm in my last year at St Hilda's, by the way."

"I say! There's a coincidence! Why haven't we met? David — " he called to his companion — "the young lady's from Oxford, too. Apparently we have a lady locum in old Gray's place.

This is a friend, David Yates. He visits his grandparents in Greendales for Christmas, though he's a southerner by birth. He comes for the hunt and the ball and all the jollification we can muster in our neck of the woods."

Candida liked what she heard more and more, and the voice was so refined, so sure of itself.

"I say," it went on, "we don't know your name."

"I'm sorry. Stupid of me. Candida Devine. How d'you do."

Her little hand was shaken twice.

"I say!" Jeremy's favourite expression. "I'll bet they all tell you Devine by name and divine by nature, eh?"

"They do. I'm used to jokes about my name."

"Sorry!"

"Don't be." At last Candida smiled, showing small, exquisite teeth. "About my being met, I don't think so. My sister's a working girl and I'll just have to get a taxi."

"I say! Not likely. We'll see you to

the doctor's house. I hope we'll see much more of you, too, unless you have other plans?"

"I have no plans. I'm on my way to Greendales purely by a fluke. Actually, I was asked to go on a skiing holiday by some Oxford friends, but there was a car accident and two of them are in hospital, not hurt seriously but inconveniently. The trip was called off, of course."

"Naturally. Well, their loss is Greendales' gain. What do you say, David?"

"I think Miss Devine must be an asset to any place."

Candida looked into the second young man's countenance for the first time. His hair was dark red and his eyes a reddish brown. He was shorter, squarer than his companion but emanated a sharper masculinity.

"Are you at Queen's, too?" she asked.

"No. I'm at New College, but I expect I'll go into the army. My grandfather is General Yates. Is your sister anything like you?"

"I don't think so. In any case, she's much older than I am. By the way, call me Candy."

"I say!" Jeremy thought he had been ignored long enough. "What luck running into you! We're almost there, by the way, so gather your monkeys and parrots, all. Leave the heavy stuff to me, Candy."

Candida accepted David's hand to step down to the platform when the train stopped. She felt her hand squeezed slightly and those reddish eyes raked hers briefly before they were joined by Jeremy.

A tall figure paused by the trio briefly, having come from the second-class part of the train. He was tall, almost lean, shabbily dressed and very fair, with light grey eyes.

"Hello, you two! Home again?"

"Hello, Toby. Regards to all at the Rectory. Miss Devine — our Rector's son, Toby Soames."

Again glances were exchanged, baby-blue eyed on Candida's part, critical and faintly disapproving on the newcomer's before he went off with a slight nod.

"Toby's a curate in Leeds. Not quite of our ilk, but we've known him all our lives. Ah! Here's Wilkes, so our transport is waiting. Good lad, Wilkes! We're dropping the young lady at Crag Lee. This is her luggage. Come along, my dear Candy! You pick the bits and pieces up, Dave, if you want a lift, you lazy toad."

★ ★ ★

For once Nancy's surgery had been large and things had gone rather slowly. The first snow of the winter had melted leaving slush-filled ditches and a raw, wet wind which was producing a crop of sore throats and wheezing chests. There was nothing really serious apart from one young girl who was dismissed back home to stay in bed and await the workings of the antibiotics prescribed for her.

"See she stays in bed, Mrs Thurrock, or she could have a roaring bronchitis by Christmas. I'm sorry about the school play but they'll just have to find another Mary."

"Oh, Mum! Oh, Doctor!"

"I know, Kathie, but your health must come first."

"I'll see to that, Doctor. She's always had a paper chest has our Kathie."

Finally Nancy entered up the last treatment card and wearily took off her white coat. She expected her dinner would have been left on the hot-plate, as Don's side of the waiting-room had been empty for some time. She was surprised, therefore, to hear a woman's voice coming from the dining-room and then Don's amused laughter. She opened the door hardly daring to believe and then said, "Candy! Oh, my darling, you came! No word. Why?"

"Thought I'd surprise you. Don and I have had a couple of aperitifs. What will you have? You look a rag, old thing."

Nancy promptly felt like a rag against her young sister, who was wearing a fashionable blue wool dress which complimented her shining eyes.

"Nancy comes back to life on dry sherry," Don said, pouring out the pale liquid and handing it to his colleague. "We waited dinner for you. What a surgery you had tonight!"

"Yes, the biggest yet. I hope we're not going to have an epidemic of flu before Christmas."

"Now you two are not to talk shop," Candida said sharply. "You can do that when I'm not here."

Don smiled indulgently at her. She was an eye-catcher and like any man he enjoyed looking at pretty things. Nancy saw him doing it quite a lot as she served up the pot-roast Mrs Waddell had left in the slow cooker, and felt a little niggle of pure feminine jealousy which she suppressed as being unworthy. Candy might have been expected to look travel-worn, but she was absolutely blooming and seemed prepared to chatter away all night.

"I was shown my room, by the way, by your housekeeper before she left," Candy volunteered. "I apologized for coming on spec, so to speak, but she said the guest-room was always ready and she switched on an enormous electric blanket so I shall be very cosy. I must say I'm impressed with your new billet, Nancy. Very impressed. A great improvement on the old one."

"Oh? I thought you might find us a bit dull."

"I haven't had a dull moment up to now. After meeting Jeremy and David on the train, who brought me here, I had barely seen my room when Don appeared and he has been entertaining me." She flashed him one of her smiles. "By the way, I hope you don't mind, Sis, but I've arranged a little drinks party for tomorrow night. You're both very welcome to come."

At last Nancy met Don's eyes. His

were ruefully amused while hers blazed momentarily.

"A party, here?" Nancy asked.

"Well, why not? You said I was to consider any place you worked at as my home. I've asked the two boys I met and told them to bring along any of their friends and a few girls. It'll just be drinks and maybe a few sausages on sticks and nuts and things. It's a way of getting to know people. Don't worry about the catering. I'll see to all that if you can lend me a few pounds. By the way, I bought some smashing boots on my credit card. I'm a bit short of cash and must dun you again. But you don't want me to look like a sloven, do you, Nancy?"

Don said quickly, "Well, I can see this is family talk so I'll go off to my place. I'll be glad to call in at your party, Candy, tomorrow. It should quite brighten the old house up. I'll bring a couple of bottles."

Nancy was looking daggers at him

as he winked and said goodnight.

"He's really enjoying all this," she thought, "Candy showing off and me being the old ugly sister. I love her but I could throttle her cheerfully at this moment. I've been here three months and after a couple of hours she's more at home than I am."

★ ★ ★

Nancy didn't think a drinks party for the younger element of the village would be much in her line, and Candy had dropped a hint that she needn't feel obliged to stay and chaperone if she had anything better to do, but she decided that she would at least put in an early appearance and welcome the guests to Crag Lee alongside her sister. She hadn't intended doing much dressing up for the occasion, either, until she saw Candida in a strapless watered silk creation which shone through violet to palest blue depending on the light. The younger girl looked lovely but Nancy pounced.

"Candy, just how many clothes have you bought recently? How much is it going to cost me? I'm not making our fortune, you know, and if we're going to buy a flat somewhere I need to save up."

"Would you have me wear sackcloth? I have to have clothes. I only had two dreary evening gowns for college dinner evenings and I've rung the changes with scarves and belts and things until I got fed up. I bought this dress, and a lemon chiffon one, in a sale, if you must know. Dead cheap. Two hundred pounds the two, and as I know the shopgirl I needn't pay till I get back to Oxford."

Nancy's head was ringing. Two hundred pounds for dresses, eighty pounds for boots, no doubt another hundred for undies and taradiddles.

"Don't nag," she warned herself as she could have screamed at the spendthrift. "All right," she forced herself to say. "But that's the lot for a while, I hope. I suppose I'd better dress up a bit."

"Have you been on a spending spree?"

"No. It'll have to be some old thing I've had for years."

But Nancy had always possessed excellent dress sense and, knowing Don was calling in, she didn't want to look like Candy's maiden aunt, so she searched through her things and decided to wear her black dress with the silver flashes down each side. Being fair the dress loved her, and she did her hair in a different style, a youthful style, brushed over from right to left with a small arrow-shaped silver pin holding it in place.

Candida took one look and demanded, "Have I seen you in that before?"

"I don't know. But I've worn it before. I've had it at least five years."

"Well, that accounts for it. It's too young for you."

"Oh, come off it, dear! I'm not

exactly decrepit."

"No, but you are nearly thirty and you don't look it in that dress."

"Well, I'm sure you didn't mean that as a compliment, but I feel encouraged. In any case I'm only just twenty-eight so don't put years on me. You need a shawl, or something. When you open the door winter will blast in."

"I'm wearing no shawl. What an idea!"

Nancy rather enjoyed her young sister's obvious disapproval of her appearance, which meant she sensed a rival presence, and this was supported when the first guests arrived, who were Jeremy Huntley and a rather precious girl home from finishing school in Switzerland, Fiona Richards, who looked like a baby doll and couldn't sound her rs.

"Hey, Doc!" Jeremy said as he was introduced. "What a surprise *you* are! I can see I'm not going to be very well this vac. Fiona, this is our new doc."

"Hello, Fiona! Jeremy. I must warn

you I have a large supply of very blunt, slow-acting hypodermics for anyone caught wasting *my* valuable time."

There was laughter in which Candida did not join. She said, ignoring Fiona after the first hand touching, "Do come and help me with the drinks, Jeremy."

Nancy shepherded the girl to a chair and brought her a sweet martini.

"I didn't catch your surname, Fiona."

"Wichards. My father's the MFH and ve'y busy organizing the Boxing Day meet. You look too young to be a doctor. Are you weally?"

"Yes, and all those years of training must show somewhere. Ah! more guests. Will you excuse me?"

This time she was subjected to the intense, speculative stare of Adam, in the figure of David Yates, whose predatory instincts were aroused by these newcomers to the district. He had brought his two sisters, both quite plain but full of girlish chatter and giggles. He clung rather a long time to Nancy's hand but she had grown expert in her

147

hospital training days at freeing herself from unwanted attentions and was quite happy to pass him on to Candy and take the girls under her wing. There were soon eleven youngsters present and — the carpet having been taken up in the large drawing-room the music-centre began to blare out, Jeremy had brought his collection of pop records with him, and feet began to shuffle on the wood-block floor.

"Another ten minutes and I'll leave them to it," Nancy was thinking, when Don arrived, announcing that he had brought a guest. Nancy thought it must be Sister Temple, but it was a young man, not in DJ as the others were but wearing a leather-elbowed tweed jacket over a green pullover.

Don made the introduction. The Reverend Toby Soames, son of the rector, home for Christmas.

"Toby came for a game of chess but I told him we'd better show up here for a drink or two first, as I'd promised."

"You're very welcome, Toby," Nancy

said, liking the looks of this clean-cut fair-haired young cleric. "How's your mother? I hope the linctus I gave her is helping?"

"Thank you, Dr Devine. She isn't complaining, just croaking a little."

Candida came over.

"Why, Don dear!" she gushed. "And — and you again," she said to Toby, somehow managing to make her blue eyes turn into glass. "May I get you a drink, or don't you, apart from communion wine?"

The taunt was too studied and Nancy wanted to shake her sister.

"Oh, I do, in moderation, Miss Devine. Sherry if I may, please."

He followed Candy to the buffet where she handed him a glass with bare civility.

"He must be a glutton for punishment," Nancy observed. "My sweet little sister just told him to go away and play somewhere else, in her own inimitable way."

"Don't worry about Toby. He can

take care of himself. How about a drink for me?"

"Of course. *And* me. I haven't had anything yet. This must be the rowdiest Crag Lee has ever been. Is it annoying you?"

"No, of course not. So long as it's only once in a very long while."

"I can promise you that. Gin-and-lime?"

"Tonic, please. Here's to your big, brown eyes."

"Oh!" she smiled tremulously. "That was unexpected with all this youth and beauty present. Thanks, and cheers!"

# 7

IN Candida's opinion her little 'drinks party' had been a great success. She had been invited to watch the hunt on Boxing Day from the Huntley's Land-Rover, and then join the family and friends for lunch before coming home to Crag Lee to prepare for the Hunt Ball in the evening, which was reputed to go on nearly all night. The occasions appealed to her with her gift for show-womanship, tremendously, but she was beginning to find Jeremy Huntley, who also had a very good opinion of himself, a bit of a twit. Alone in a corner with David Yates she was much more conscious of an animal magnetism surging between them which was rather delicious. Aware that he could not compete with the local high event of the season, he had cast his net to steal a march on his college friend. He had asked Candida to dine with him the next evening but one at a rather special place, and she had hesitated only long enough not to appear too eager. While their two heads, fair and copper were close together, Don decided to refill his and Nancy's glasses.

"Your sister is — er — hum! — ah, pretty worldly wise, I gather?" he asked awkwardly, slopping his own drink.

Nancy smiled.

"If you mean does she know about the birds and the bees, who doesn't, nowadays, at twenty-one?"

"I suppose it's no business of mine, but young David, there, got one of his grandfather's servant girls into trouble. There's a child and the old man supports the pair, who now live in another village. I just thought I'd mention that."

Nancy looked at Candida, now leaving the said young seducer for her other guests, but looking back at him with a knowing smile.

"I don't think Candy's a loose girl," she said at last. "But one has to hope for the best. I can't afford to worry about her when she's at Oxford. I have to believe in her. She's my sister."

"Well said!"

The next time Nancy looked Candy was talking with Toby Soames, or was she arguing with him? Her eyes flashed and she was rocking from foot to foot as he spoke.

"Very well," Nancy heard her say. "I'll call in at the Rectory and hear what your father has to say on the subject. But I'm not at all religious. I can tell you that from the start."

"How can you be so sure, so young?"

"I'm not all that young. I have a mind trained to deal with facts."

Nancy lost the trend after that and apologized to Don so that she could go and chat to the neglected females at the party. She was glad when things began to break up and Don persuaded a rather florid youth, Tom Brandon, to help him replace the carpet and furniture. Nancy went off to wash the glasses while Candida's goodbyes were protracted at the front door.

Don said goodnight and went off with Toby for a late game of chess. Candy appeared in the kitchen and said, "What're *you* doing? That's what Mrs Waddell's paid for."

"Not to wash up after your parties. She has enough to do. I don't mind. You go off to bed if you want."

"It was quite a success, wasn't it? I got loads of invitations. I may go up to Aviemore for some skiing at New Year if I can stand that Brandon boy's company. Apparently he's been skiing since he was four and has an almost brand-new Porche. Everybody here seems to be somebody. It's a very select area, isn't it?"

"Well, I see some of its other facets, the old and sick, who don't go to parties and Hunt Balls, and — "

"Oh! don't bore me with your working schedules, sis. There are old and sick everywhere. You can't expect every young person to worry about them. Nobody here, tonight, cared a fig for these other people you mention."

"Maybe Toby Soames did."

"Oh, him! I don't count him."

"No. I don't expect you do with all those DJed dummies paying court to you."

"There's no need to insult my guests because they know how to dress for occasions."

"You mean because they can afford to dress for occasions, don't you? Anyway, I'm sorry I sneered. If you enjoyed your party that's really all that's important, and I'm glad your vac looks like being quite lively. I had thought you'd find Greendales a bit flat, but you have magnetized all the bright young things, like a female Pied Piper, to follow at your beck. There! the kitchen looks tidier, now, and no breakages. Did I hear you arranging to go to the Rectory?"

"Yes. Toby Soames got me into an argument and was really enjoying seeing me struggling to put my case. He says his father enjoys a good discussion so I said I'd join him in one. I wasn't afraid."

Nancy smiled secretly. At the moment Candida professed to be an atheist, but she was as determined to enjoy Christmas as anyone else, especially the receiving of gifts and the celebrations accruing.

"Right!" said Nancy. "I think I'll go to bed. I'm on standby duty tomorrow."

"What does that mean?"

"Well, all the doctors in the area take it in turns to be on call on Sundays. My turn's tomorrow."

★ ★ ★

Nancy was called out only twice on the Sunday, and arrived back at Crag Lee to find herself squashed to a sturdy masculine chest in a suffocating embrace. She had only time to gasp before her lips were seized and what breath she had left was drawn from her so that eventually she had to struggle with her arms and literally push her partner in this enterprise away.

"Barry! So you've come! But do you *have* to be so rough?"

"Darling, darling Nancy! I've missed you. There's a lot of making up to be done." Once more Nancy's protestations were drowned as strong lips silenced hers.

"Oh! sorry," came from behind them and Nancy realized Don had come upon them and retreated as quickly.

"Will you stop it?" Nancy now demanded almost angrily. "Barry, I had all this out with you before I left London. I'm fond of you and we can be good pals, but nothing more. You're not even in love with me. You just enjoy rugby tackles with females."

"Cross my heart and hope to die, Nancy, I've fretted for you more than I could ever have imagined. I do have a heart, you know, under all this brawn, and I seem to think I offered it to you on a platter."

"Yes, and you took a red-headed nurse off to an all-night party while I was considering my verdict. You couldn't just be true to one woman if you tried, Barry. I'm probably only desirable because I absented myself. No! Not again! I've had a rough two hours dealing with a scalding case and getting the woman into hospital. I need a reviving cup of tea."

"That chap's making one. It's probably ready."

"Anyway," Nancy was removing her warm coat and gloves, "why didn't you phone you were on your way?"

"I did. I phoned from Cawnpore — "

"From where?" asked Nancy.

"Well, wherever it is one gets off the train. Your sweet little sister answered, saying she was just on her way out with somebody and handed me over to that chap, who offered to come and pick me up. Very civil of him."

"His name's Donald Wayne, Don for short."

"Yes. We introduced ourselves. He got me in at the Dog and Duck and then brought me on here. You've got a nice set-up. Lovely country. I'll enjoy my week's leave. I refuse to believe you've forgotten all we once meant to each other and I shall try to refresh your memory. What changed you was the shock of your parents' death. You should be getting over that a bit now, however."

"Tea," Nancy said firmly, hearing the rattle of cups from the drawing-room. "Hello, Don!" she greeted, trying not to look as though she had just been kissed and crushed nearly to death, though her colour was heightened by the sheer embarrassment of having been caught in the act. She had told Don she and Barry were just good friends. How must he think she behaved with friends of the opposite sex?

"There's the cup that cheers," Don offered promptly, as she sat down by the roaring fire. "Sugar for you?" he asked Barry.

"Yes, please. Though life's much sweeter in prospect for me, now," and he gave one of those tawny-eyed looks at Nancy, which made her want to creep under the table.

"I've turned the slow cooker on," Don said quickly, "as per Mrs Waddell's instructions and your dinner will be ready, about eight. There's a cold custard tart for desert."

"Will you be in for dinner?"

"No. As you're on call have it tète-a-tète this first evening with your — friend. I'm dining at the Rectory. I realized Dr Humphries — I may call you Barry — ?"

"Sure, Don. We're not stuffed shirts, are we?"

" — might miss not having a car while he's here, so I thought of young Toby who has an elderly, but serviceable Triumph Herald. He handed over the keys like a shot and glad to oblige."

"So I have transport, a lodging, my girl — I lack nothing," Barry said triumphantly. "They're damned civil round here, not like the uncaring citizens of the metropolis. You've landed on your feet, Nancy."

"I do work," she reminded him. "Quite hard, in fact. Apart from two surgeries most days there are the home visits and the pps and it's a very sprawling practice. I seem to spend ages in the car. It must be worse for Don as he has more patients than I. Also we're both on duty over Christmas. We just happened to draw the short straw this year. You and Candy may have to keep each other company on Christmas Day if we're called out."

"Well, that should be seasonally interesting. Candy had no good will to offer me. I may go out and climb this crag of yours, weather permitting."

"On the other hand, we may get off luckily. I'm chief cook and bottle-washer. I'm cooking the turkey. We must just wait and see and make things as festive as we can."

"I'd like to mention," said Don, "that I asked Myra to join us for lunch on Boxing Day, if that's all right with you, Nancy?"

"Of course it is. That means we'll be a foursome as Candy is lunching at the Hall. Will Sister Temple be watching the hunt?"

"I know she'd like to. She was disappointed when I said I couldn't take her. Maybe Barry could act as escort? Myra never likes going anywhere on her own."

"Before I commit myself, who is Myra?" Barry asked watchfully.

"A friend of mine," Don said quickly. "A very attractive brunette and a Sister from Kendal Hospital."

"Well, certainly I'll stand in for you, old chap. A long time since I saw a real meet. Is it a horseback affair or John Peel style, on foot?"

"Oh, horses, a pack of hounds, the real Tally-ho stuff. All very spectacular. Would you like to go, Nancy, if I hold the fort? After all, you haven't seen the hunt either."

"No, thanks. There'll be other meetings, won't there? We're on duty as a partnership so I'll stay with you. In any case, I have lunch to prepare."

"Well, I'll leave you. You must have loads to talk about."

"Absolute loads," Barry agreed.

Oh! Nancy almost prayed. If only he meant we were just going to talk!

She watched Don leave with some regret. Funny how her feelings had changed towards him. She couldn't define them but she felt they were at last on the same wavelength, that he understood her quandaries and sympathised with her problems. She could talk to him, nowadays, and they had discovered they shared the same sense of humour. They laughed a lot together. She almost resented that they were not being allowed to share their Christmas duty unencumbered by other people. She would have enjoyed coming back and finding him there after an emergency call and telling him all about it, as she would have welcomed his return home and confiding in her. But there was Candy and now Barry and Sister Temple to be made welcome on Boxing Day.

Ah! well! Better gird herself for the next assault by Barry. She went back into the drawing-room after letting Don out and found her ex-love examining a snapshot.

"That chap must have dropped this out of his wallet. He changed me a cheque. Could this be Sister Temple?"

Nancy looked and said, "Yes, that is she."

Barry gazed lasciviously back at the picture in his hand.

"Quite a cracker, isn't she?"

"Yes. But kindly remember she is *his* cracker."

"You mean that chap's?"

"Don't keep saying that chap! His name's Don."

"All right, don't sound so crotchety.

They're that way about each other, are they?"

"I don't know. They were once engaged but I think it was broken off. They do see a lot of each other, however. I'll go and stir the pot in the kitchen. Dinner shouldn't be too long. Leave that picture on the side-table so that Don sees it when he comes in."

★ ★ ★

The next day, as Nancy had her surgeries and calls to make, Barry climbed the fell and amused himself. He took Nancy to dine at the Dog and Duck when she was free. She tried confiding in him, telling him of her problem 'child', Lily Hulme.

"I gave her her Christmas present today, a large colouring book and pencils. She was quite happy until I told her that her sister was very ill and might die; just lately I've discussed with her how awful it is when pets die, and make us grieve, and she told me

165

of a kitten she had had which died in her arms and made her cry for weeks. Her old nanny, Mrs Jenkins, told me that Lily had actually crushed the kitten to death. She doesn't know her own strength. Well, the last report on Miss Pansy, her sister, wasn't at all encouraging so I thought I'd better warn Lily what might happen. She has a lisp, and she looked at me with staring eyes and said, 'If Panthy dieth it ith your fault. Thee wath all right until you took her away. You were naughty to take her away. I'll pay you back.' Honestly, Barry, she's like a big kid but she frightens me. I think we ought to get her into a special hospital before Pansy dies."

"Yes, my dearest, but need this demented woman spoil our dinner date? I didn't come to Greendales to talk shop."

"No, of course not. I'm sorry. It isn't as if you can help in any way. I'll have the Aylesbury duckling, if I may."

The meal was good but Nancy kept

wishing it wasn't Barry sitting across from her. Although he had asked her not to talk about her problems in the practice he was only too eager to bore her with his feats on the rugby field.

"I scored two tries against St Charles' Hospital and both were converted. Our team had given up when we were eight points down at half-time so I gave them a bit of a nag. 'You look like a lot of lost dogs with their tails down in the mud,' I said. 'We can do it if you'll just show a bit more willing. Fair means or foul so long as the ref doesn't see.' So after that it was child's play. I had the ball and nobody was going to stop me. I charged down two of the blighters and — are you listening, Nancy?"

"Yes, Barry. I'm sorry. I fancied I saw Candy and her escort over there, but it isn't her. As you were saying?"

"Well, we won. I did it again from a long throw in and our tails were up for a change. You'd have been proud of me."

Nancy wondered. Barry was rough.

Rough with a woman and a menace to his opponents on the sporting field. Being rough was his way of showing his masculinity, she supposed. He was like a great gale of wind that one day would blow itself out.

Back at Crag Lee, approaching midnight, she grew tired of resisting him and submitted to his embraces. After all, it was Don who had remarked she had been living like a nun all these weeks.

She eventually stirred and smoothed herself down, however.

"Barry, I'm tired! I wish Candy was back."

"Oh! Let the kid have her fun."

"I don't mind fun but her escort happens to be the father of an illegitimate child."

"Well! well! So we have our scandals in Greendales, too, do we?"

"I suppose it was a scandal at the time. A simple servant girl being forced to go away and live in another village with her child. That young man is a sex menace. I knew it when he was squeezing my hand. Now he's with Candy and it's — it's nearly one-thirty. What *are* they doing?"

"Your little sister is an adult and intelligent, my little prude. She's no simple servant-girl. She's probably having a damned good time. Why don't I stay tonight, and we can have one, too?"

Nancy looked at him painedly. "Oh, Barry, you never stop trying, do you? It has to mean more to me than a cheap thrill. It's the way I'm made. I thought I had always made that abundantly clear to you. I think you should be going. Won't they have locked up at the pub?"

"I have a back-door key. I dropped a hint I might be quite late. But I'm beginning to get the message that you are having to try very hard to tolerate my company. You really meant it when you said we were through, didn't you? And I, poor fool, thought you were merely under emotional stress."

"Barry, I have never deceived you.

I said we could be friends, but we obviously can't. You want a woman physically."

"Well, of course I do. Is that so odd?"

"No. But it can't be me."

"I'm repulsive to you?"

"No! Why do you try to put the wrong words in my mouth? I like you. We've had some good times together. But now it's boiling down to the one thing between us and I can't enjoy it. I'm sorry."

"Oh, plenty pebbles on the beach, my dear Nancy. If you want to grow into a dried-up lemon, more interested in your doctoring than human relationships, well go ahead! I promise you no more bashing of my ugly fat head against a brick wall."

"Oh, Barry, now you're making me feel awful. You're not ugly. Quite the reverse. Some other woman will tell you so much better than I can. Ah! that must be Candy. She's back!"

"She's been between us all evening,

probably having her fun without a thought for us."

Candida, however, looked more brittle than happy. She could scarcely be civil to the two regarding her.

"Hello! Waiting for me, sis? I'm a big girl, now, and I'm going to bed. Goodnight, both!"

"Something's wrong," said Nancy. "You'd better go, Barry. I want to talk to her."

"She's an unexploded bomb if I know one. I'd keep far enough away from her. Anyhow, thanks for your company, Nancy. I won't be along tomorrow, but I'll turn up Christmas Day so as not to embarrass you."

"Don't be hurt, Barry."

"Hurt? Me? I'm tough as old rugby boots. Don't worry about me."

Nancy locked up and raced up to Candy's room. She could hear the girl muttering angrily as she undressed, throwing shoes about.

"May I come in?" Nancy almost begged. "What's the matter, Candy?

171

Haven't you had a pleasant evening? I don't mean to be nosey — "

"Then don't be!"

Nancy turned away and Candy's voice grew softer. "Sorry, sis. I didn't mean to take it out on you. Actually, it started off a lovely evening, gorgeous meal, generous compliments from my companion, dancing cheek to cheek. Then, when the witching hour had struck, I was quite sleepy — we'd had a lot of wine with our meal and drinks before, and I just wanted to get home and go to bed. It's snowing — did you know? — looks like being a white Christmas. We'd come about a mile and then the damned car stopped. Dave was under the bonnet, all over the place, and we were in a lonely lane. He finally said he couldn't deal with the trouble in the dark and were miles from a garage and we'd better make ourselves comfy in the back under some rugs. Well, *I* didn't know where we were so I complied. It was only when he started that I became suspicious; a few kisses and cuddles I expected but he was on an assault course in no time. I hit him where it hurt and said I'd walk to a garage if he wouldn't. I wasn't born yesterday and in the back of a car on a snowy night? He *had* to be joking. Finally he pretended to find a torch on the floor, looked under the bonnet again and — wonder of wonders! — found the trouble in five minutes flat. I gave him a piece of my mind, I can tell you, and it only took us ten minutes to get here after that. How can young men be so crass? It beats me. I'm no prude, but if I'm ever seduced it will have to be with much more finesse than that, and not in the back of a damned car. Oh, good! You remembered to put my blanket on. Goodnight, sis!"

"Goodnight, Candy. Have a lie-in in the morning — Christmas Eve. I have one surgery, that's all, and a few comforts to deliver to my old chronics. May I — kiss you?"

"Oh, you sentimental old thing! Of course."

Nancy went off to her own bed, knowing that she'd be tired in the morning but that — with her mind easy — she'd sleep well for what remained of the night. She felt glad that Master Dave had received his come-uppance, and she was quite proud of Candy for dealing it out.

# 8

CHRISTMAS DAY at Crag Lee was really quite pleasant. The previous evening Don had brought in a small potted tree and fished out the family's box of decorations from the loft. Nancy and Candy had dressed the tree, Nancy smiling behind her hand as her supposedly atheistic sister tenderly set out the crib and its attendant figures underneath the lowest spreading branches and then stood back to admire her handiwork.

Next day Mrs Waddell wasn't coming, or on Boxing Day, but Nancy was really surprised when there was a tap on her bedroom door and Don entered with a tray of tea on which was a single rose in a glass.

"Well, thanks! How did *you* get in?"

"I have my own key. Thought I must

get the chief cook up. That turkey is some size."

"But it's all prepared. I only have to turn the oven on. Still, thanks. It's time I was moving."

"Now, I'll take a tray to your sister. By the way, I see Santa Claus has been."

Nancy didn't question him further. She had placed a few parcels under the tree last night, and when she eventually went downstairs she saw that there was quite a mound. Don was making coffee and toast in the huge kitchen as she donned a kitchen overall and turned on the gas in the oven to cook the turkey.

"Quite a domestic scene," she remarked. "That coffee smells good."

"Oh, I'm quite house-trained," he told her. "I could do you bacon and eggs if you would prefer — "

"No, thanks. I've managed at long last to stop Mrs Waddell feeding me up like a fighting cock. Toast is fine with home-made marmalade. I see our snow is still lying."

"Yes, and it's damned cold out. The wind is what is known locally as thin. Let's hope everybody in our neck of the woods keeps well today and all the busy housewives watch out for burning fat."

Candy came in wearing a dressing-gown. "Oh, hello, Don! I thought it was Santa had brought me that heavenly pot of tea to bed. Why aren't you married? You're just the sort I could fall for if you were five years younger. You're nice, good-looking, thoughtful and very sexy."

"Candy!" Nancy protested.

"But five years too old, eh?" Don insisted on laughing. "Hard luck for me. I must consider having a face-lift."

"You're all right as you are," Nancy told him, sipping coffee. "My sister has a nasty habit of making people feel geriatric."

When they paused for mid-morning sherry and a mince-pie, parcels were opened. Nancy was surprised how many packages there were from grateful patients, which Don had had squirrelled away to keep for the great day; there were hand-embroidered handkerchiefs, a pretty bed-jacket, a jar of home-made treacle toffee and a lovely woolly scarf, and so many cards she couldn't count. Candy had bought her a new umbrella, pale pink and see-through, and Don had bought perfume for both sisters.

"I'd better baste the turkey," said Nancy, as Candy draped herself under some mistletoe for a kiss of thanks. She had deliberately avoided the mistletoe after finding Don eyeing her speculatively whenever she went in that direction. She had an idea that Don's kiss, even though only a token gesture of the season, would stir something in her she wouldn't want to be aroused to clamour in her unsatisfied thereafter.

Barry arrived shortly afterwards, bearing gifts and offering kisses to the girls, though Nancy had to admit his salute for her was almost brotherly.

Candy, trying on new suede gloves, was being very nice to Barry and offering him a drink, while Nancy had to occupy herself in the kitchen, preparing vegetables.

Everybody wanted to look at the turkey, spurting out its juices into a deep tray and smelling deliciously, when the telephone rang.

"Ah!" said Don. "I'll get that. Baby with a high temp," he came back into the kitchen to announce. "I'd better go see, though it may only be chickenpox, which has broken out in Carnforth. I hope to be back for lunch."

"Which won't be before two o'clock," Nancy told him. "We'll wait for you. Did we get any crackers, Don?"

"Yes. They're on the sideboard."

She watched him wrapping up warmly to go out, really caring that the pleasant little party they were having was being interrupted.

"Take care on the roads," she advised seriously.

All in a moment he had swooped

179

and she was being kissed in a way a woman likes to be kissed, so that needles of awareness shot through her being deliciously.

"Oh, you — !" she said to cover her confusion, and looked up to see the mistletoe. "I'm a mile away," she told him.

"Near enough," he smiled at her. "See you later."

There were no more calls that day and the meal was really delicious, so that everybody ate well and drank sufficiently to be satisfied to sit by the roaring fire and watch television, which was very entertaining that Christmas Day. Barry had evidently taken her words to heart and he did not even touch her as they sat side by side on the big sofa. He was civil, he was pleasant, but not at all familiar. Candy became somewhat bored as the evening wore on, and began to yawn, and by ten o'clock both men left.

"Well, I think I'll go to bed," said a tired Nancy. "I'll switch the phone through in case there's a call."

"Oh," Candy had perked up a little. "There's a film I want to see. So I'll say goodnight, sis."

Nancy did not fall asleep immediately. She remembered that kiss and thrilled again and again. "Just what I didn't want to happen," she told herself. "Another woman's fiancé with the power to make me feel like Cleopatra. There's no future in it. It doesn't mean anything to him."

Yet now he had done it to her twice, the night of the concert and again today. She must avoid such situations and try to forget they were attractive elements, which was easier said than done.

★ ★ ★

Boxing Day was as unlike the previous day in events which took place as could be. All that was similar to Nancy was that she was again in charge of the kitchen, though on this occasion the turkey would be served cold with the hot vegetables and gravy she had to prepare. Don came to ask if he could help, as Candy had gone off blithely with Jeremy Huntley early on to take her place in the Hall Land-Rover to follow the hunt in comfort, but Nancy dismissed him with thanks.

"You give our guests a drink when they arrive, Don," she said. "I suppose they'll be rushing off to see the hunt. Ah! There's somebody arrived."

Sister Temple and Barry arrived together, obviously having introduced themselves on the doorstep. They were drinking sherry, still in their outdoor things, when Nancy entered the drawing-room. Barry raised his hand in her direction, nothing more, and Myra Temple said, "So you're head cook and bottle-washer, eh? Dr Devine? A change of occupation for you."

"Quite a welcome one," Nancy agreed, "though the real job must come first if there are any calls. Don will have told you we're covering the district for these two days?"

"Yes. Which is quite a bore for you, I'm sure."

"Will you excuse us?" asked Barry. "If we're to see this hunt, Myra, we'd better get moving. See you two at feeding-time."

Nancy was pouring herself a sherry, and observed, "Barry makes friends very easily."

"About a minute and a half I made it," Don said drily, "and Myra was more than ready."

"Still, it's a friendly time of year," Nancy went on, "and they've only gone to watch a hunt. There'll be hundreds there."

"I don't mind if you don't," Don said. "He's your — er — friend."

"And she's yours. No, I don't mind." Nancy didn't, only so far as she knew that all between her and Barry was over and he could readily be on the hunt — not a fox-hunt this time — again. His masculine ego demanded he should have females admiring him, and Myra Temple's gaze had not been disinterestedly upon him at any time.

Don was called out shortly afterwards, and then Nancy had to follow, leaving the Ansafone turned on, to make sure one of her elderly patients had not hurt herself unduly by falling out of bed. The old lady was surrounded by caring relatives, however, and was only shaken with a slightly bruised hip. There were no breaks, no great areas of pain. "Give her a brandy or a whisky," Nancy advised the eldest daughter of the family, "whichever she prefers, and tuck the bedclothes well in so it can't happen again. After the holiday I'll arrange for her to have a cot with raised sides, if you like."

"Mother's nearly ninety," the daughter said. "You do whatever you can, Doctor, to keep her safe."

Back at Crag Lee Don was back switching on the tape-recorder in the study.

"Just one call, here," he announced. "A member of the hunt with a suspected broken leg after a toss. I'll call the ambulance and get over there, pronto, though the St John's Ambulance people are usually in attendance for first aid. See you!"

"It looks like being one of those days," Nancy decided as she started the vegetables off on a low heat and set the table for lunch in the dining-room.

All looked very nice. She had managed to cut some Christmas roses and winter jasmine with which to decorate the long table and with the shining cutlery and sparkling glasses all looked charmingly festive.

Once again the phone rang and she answered it to hear an anxious mother reporting that one of her earrings was missing after being last seen clutched in baby's warm little hand.

"I think he's swallowed it, Doctor. He's very whingy and whiny."

"Don't worry, Mrs Forrest. What sort of earring was it?"

"Just a plain gold ring. The screw

had broken off and I was going to get it mended."

"How old is Baby John?"

"Fourteen months."

"Then give him a rusk or a couple of biscuits. If he's swallowed the earring that should help it to pass through his system."

"You mean — ?"

"I mean let nature take its course, Mrs Forrest. If it has gone in then it will surely come out. Just watch closely for a day or two."

"You mean you're not coming?"

"If baby's in real pain of course I'll come. But at the moment I don't think there's any need. He's probably whinging for his dinner and may sleep all afternoon. But if you're still worried, later on, do call me back."

"Really!" Nancy thought as she strode back to the kitchen. "Some people would have you in as great a panic as they get into. The things I've seen babies pass in my time! and that's not all that long."

The visitors returned just before Don, still obviously on the best of terms. By the time Don had filled in details of the accident he had attended in the house-log, lunch was ready for serving.

"Let's hope we can get our meal in peace," Nancy decided. "I don't know about anybody else but I'm hungry."

Don carved, Nancy served the vegetables and passed the gravy and Barry and Myra carried on their conversation without trying to make it general. Nancy frowned as she thought Don was being a little too quiet.

"Sorry I haven't any crackers today," Nancy said loudly and cheerfully. "But I somehow can't imagine this company in funny hats."

"Well certainly not me," said Sister Temple. "When I was a child, etc., but I'm sure you know the rest of it. Who was that girl you were talking to, Barry? The one who was just too pretty-pretty to be true?"

"Actually that was Nancy's sister.

She's an Oxford student and — yes — she *is* pretty."

"Pretty-pretty were the words Sister Temple used," Nancy said with an edge to her voice. "Used as she said them they sound derisory."

"Oh, sorry! I've trodden on Dr Devine's corns," and Myra Temple laughed.

"I have no corns to tread on, fortunately," Nancy returned. "Candida *is* very pretty. Only the jealous would say otherwise. More wine?"

"I'll see to that," said Don, as though realizing his colleague was really rattled. "Another very nice meal, Nancy. Thanks for all your efforts."

"There's trifle if anybody's interested?" Nancy looked round. Nobody was. "Then I'll serve the coffee in the drawing-room."

"Dear me!" Nancy heard Myra Temple say as she went kitchenwards, "I do believe I'm in the doghouse."

"Oh, Nancy doesn't bear malice," Barry felt obliged to say. "She's protective towards her kid sister, naturally."

"Well, I meant no harm."

"Of course, you didn't. Don't give it another thought."

"Or do," Don broke into the duologue, "and don't do it again. You must have been the sort of kid, Myra, who said on crowded buses, 'Oh, look at that lady in the funny hat!' and you're still at it."

"From one who knows," Myra winked at Barry. "Don't you think I'm horrid?"

"You haven't been horrid to me. I'll make my own judgments."

Nancy enjoyed her second cup of coffee and thought, "Well, the washing-up won't do itself. I'd better make a start."

The phone rang.

"I'll get it," Don went hallwards.

"We're having a busy day to make up for yesterday, it seems," Nancy observed.

Don came in looking serious.

"We'll both have to go out, Nancy," he said. "Dick Bates was out for a walk with his boy, Tim. They went up the crag with their fox-terrier bitch and it was slippery. The dog went down a hole, couldn't get out, and Tim wriggled after it. Apparently he has fallen quite a distance and may have landed on his knees, with possible impaction of hips. The father can't get down the hole or see anything, only hears the kid moan and the dog bark. It's solid rock all round. Could be a dicey business. I've sent for the fire brigade and we'd better go look-see what's to be done. I've also sent for John Cardle, who knows the crag better than anybody, and told him to bring a few strong lads with him with various tools. Wrap up well, Nancy. Are — are you two interested in coming with us?"

Barry queried Myra with his tawny eyes.

"Oh! You don't want a crowd," said Myra. "What good could we do? You go on and we'll hope you get the little beggar out."

"OK. We'll take my car," said Don, switching on the Ansafone as he passed it. Nancy was well wrapped up and he had a trespassing thought; if Candida was pretty then Nancy was beautiful at times like this, all ready to do her job and eager and alive.

"Have we got everything?" he asked her, confident that she would have seen to the packing of drugs and hypodermics and dressings. "Let's hope we get that kid out before dark. He could freeze to death in that hole."

Quite soon a fleet of vehicles collected at the base of the crag, there were police, firemen, villagers who knew their countryside inside out and the trapped boy's distraught father and an uncle and grandfather, who had come to give moral support in the drama.

John Cardle, who had walked the crag since he was a child of four had little encouragement to offer.

"There's nobbut that way in, no way

out," he stared, surveying the narrow crevice dog and boy had gone down. "It's what I allus call Cardle's chimney. Lost a dog down it meself once. 'Ad to gas the poor little devil to put 'im out of 'is misery."

"The boy got down," Nancy found herself saying. "We can't gas a boy so we've got to get him out somehow."

"Well we can't blast," said John Cardle, "or we blow 'im to smithereens or kill 'im in a rockfall."

Nancy could see the boy's father covering his face in the horror of it all. Only the trapped dog could be heard barking, his din drowning whatever noise the boy was making.

"Another child could be lowered to get a rope round him?" This from a young policeman.

"Good lad, Andy," from his sergeant. "Best idea yet."

"Not good enough," Don said. "That boy could be damaged for life if he's moved before he's examined. Let's think."

"I've thought," said Nancy. "I'm not very big. I believe I could get down there. I once crept between railings when I was a medical student. Let me try. Make me a harness, please, gentlemen."

It was bitterly cold up there, with frozen snow making the rock slippery and a north-wind blowing, but Nancy took off her warm coat, scarf, cardigan and skirt and donned a harness wearing only her underclothes. Don thought how tiny she really was, and how tough. She wriggled one stockinged foot through the crevice, then the other, scraped her hips as she was lowered and then wriggled her shoulders and carefully drew her head through the widest part until there was a cheer and she was hanging in darkness. A torch was passed to her and a package of medical equipment.

"Lower away," she said, switching on the torch and noting with relief that the chimney was wider than its opening and there was now room to manoeuvre. The dog went mad upon seeing her and as she arrived straddling the young boy, promptly bit her.

"Quiet, girl! Good girl!" she said soothingly, but to the dog she was an enemy attacking her young master. Another nasty nip was the result.

"Up there!" she called. "Could you send me some sort of net down for the dog and a pair of gloves to handle her? She won't let me attend the boy."

"A sling came down on another rope and Don's own warm motoring gauntlets. With some difficulty Nancy grabbed the dog by its collar, ignoring its choking barks as she bundled it into the sling.

"Haul away!" she called and then looked at the small boy lying awkwardly on one hip. He was unconscious, but groaned slightly as Nancy ran her fingers down his damaged leg.

"In my opinion, the right femur is fractured but it's not compounded," she called up. "I'll need splints and bandages, nothing bulky."

Down came the things she needed. She gave the boy a small shot of morphia and then managed to straighten him out, there was just room on the floor of the chimney. It was difficult splinting the child as a small rock stuck out and caught her left arm every time she passed the bandage round his leg. Still she managed to forget her dog bites and her grazed shoulders and elbows. She was doing her job and, with God's help, it was going to work.

Finally she called out, "I've put my sling round his chest and tightened it. I think you can try to get him out, now. Watch it when you get to his legs. I've taken his clothes off to make things easier, so have blankets ready. OK!"

Meanwhile the firemen had erected a sheer-legs and this made the hauling easier. Nancy watched the small, practically naked figure gradually disappear through the fissure above, and a cheer followed as this was safely accomplished. Nancy began to shiver as the harness came down again, and as though some communication had taken place between herself and Don he lowered a small bottle on a string.

"Take a swig and then get that harness on quickly," he called. "I don't want you fainting. Do you hear?"

"I hear, Don," her teeth were chattering, but she put the harness round herself before drinking the warming spirit. For her to lose consciousness, now, might prove to be fatal to her. Hypothermia could kill and she was very, very cold.

She scarcely remembered being hauled upwards, or the willing hands which guided her head through the hole, then her scarred shoulders, and she didn't know the few clothes she wore were now all in tatters.

"I don't want to go to hospital," she said from Don's enveloping arms. "Take me home. Make me warm again."

"I'll look after you, you darling of a heroine, you!"

She seemed to really come to in her own bed, surrounded by hot bottles, bits of sticking plaster all over. She was wrapped in her warm, towelling-robe and drinking hot brandy and water.

"Oh, Nancy!" Candy appeared to say. "I heard what you did. I was so worried about you."

"I'll live," Nancy said, revelling in luxury. "How's the boy? Have you heard?"

"I believe he's fine. Everybody says you did well. Do you think you could sleep? I'm to let you sleep, Don says."

"You go to your ball, I'll sleep."

"Always thinking of other people. Oh, Nancy, I wish I was a bit more like you. Do you know your precious Barry and that Temple woman went off and left a houseful of dirty dishes and pans? I'm not going to the ball. I'm going to look after you for once. I'm not such a selfish brat as all that. May I send Don in before you go to sleep?"

"Do," Nancy said, drowsily content.

Don came straight over to the bed. "OK Nancy?"

"Oh, I'm much better. Thanks for everything, Don."

"*You're* thanking *me*? You're the heroine of this day's events. I'm so proud of you. So — so — oh! I can't express it. Yes, I can." He stooped and kissed her gently on the lips. "That says it best. Now I want you to sleep for twelve hours and the brandy should do the trick. I'll take both surgeries tomorrow. You stay in bed. Is that understood?"

"I don't think for once I'm going to argue."

"So goodnight, Nancy." He kissed her again.

"Goodnight, Don. I am — so very — sleepy."

# 9

NANCY never knew the exact moment when she ceased to be totally happy with her lot at Crag Lee. The day or two after the Boxing Day drama, in which she had shewn her true worth as a doctor faced with a crisis, were idyllic, not because reporters from the local press came to see her and wanted her story from anybody who would tell it, and her picture from any angle they could get it, more often than not turning away from all the attention she was receiving, but because Don was so very nice to her. It really all boiled down to that fact, and, acknowledged, Nancy had to face the fact that she had fallen more than a little in love with him, forbidden fruit though she felt him to be. Approval from Don made her day, and being with him even on the old footing of sharing their mealtimes together gilded her outlook and sharpened her appetite.

Of course she couldn't tell him she thought she was in love with him; his kisses and hugs she thought of as his way of expressing his relief and admiration for what he called her 'spunk'; they were not passionate encounters and she knew two people stood between. Don really loved Myra, and Don thought Barry loved Nancy. She did not disillusion him, and it was a relief when Barry went away and she had not even to pretend any more. It was even a relief when Candida returned to Oxford and the house felt normal again. The shouting and the tumult died down about Tim Bates' accident and Nancy visited her patients and took her surgeries and told herself not to be silly where Don was concerned. He was not for her and she was banging her head against a brick wall if she thought so.

She had also to start thinking about

her next move; in little more than eight weeks Dr and Mrs Gray would be back and she would need another job. There was not yet enough money in the bank to buy the flat she had promised Candida would be their next home, and so it meant studying the column marked *Locum Tenens Required* in the *Medical Journal*. She felt like a gipsy who must always be moving on, and on for the foreseeable future. A little cloud of depression seemed to sit over her head at this time. Nobody could see it but she was conscious of being in its shadow.

On this day she had visited the Hulme sisters. By some miracle Pansy had suddenly improved under the chemotherapy treatment she was receiving in hospital and had asked to be sent home. Nancy suspected and had been warned by the hospital specialist, that it was only a temporary improvement which could last for weeks or a month or two at the most, but Lily was openly rejoicing at having her sister back again and promised to be good; old Mrs Jenkins said she would stay and keep an eye on both sisters, for which Nancy was grateful.

She thought Don was a bit quiet over dinner that evening; she told him the news of the sisters was still good and that Mr Watkin, her multiple sclerosis sufferer, was in a period of remission and very cheerful, but he scarcely seemed to be listening.

"Have you had a bad day, Don?" she asked at length.

"No. But I have got some rather upsetting news to deliver. I had a letter from Myra today — "

"Oh?" asked Nancy, wondering what was coming next.

"She has taken a Sister's job at Dr Humphries' hospital. Apparently he told her of it and she's a pretty good nurse so she got the post. Nancy, those two have done this so they can be together. It somehow happened while they were here over Christmas and you and I might as well no longer exist for them."

Nancy felt stunned, not particularly did she mind for herself, as she had decided Barry meant nothing to her in the romantic sense, but for him to have stolen Myra Temple's affections from Don was a real blow. He must be feeling dreadfully cut up. A terrible anger suddenly blazed in her head.

"I'll write Barry and tell him exactly what I think of him," she said fiercely. "How could he be so sneaky? How dare he?"

"No, no, Nancy," Don said quickly. "Don't do anything in haste. You would sound like the typical woman scorned."

Nancy's eyes widened until she realized that Don really thought she would be writing on her own behalf, whereas the truth was she couldn't care less who Barry favoured providing it was not her friend's ex-fiancée. What had possessed her to allow Barry to come and cause all this havoc? Myra

Temple she had never liked, but if Don loved her then she felt for him. He must be going through hell and made the mistake of thinking she must be suffering similarly.

She didn't know what to say but felt depressed each time she saw Don thereafter. He would meet her eyes and glance quickly away again. They talked of patients and treatments but there was a wall between them and Nancy brooded that after she was gone Don would think of her as the girl who brought the man into his Myra's life who stole her away. She felt guilty by proxy and was often extremely unhappy about the whole situation.

Candida also stunned her by announcing her engagement.

"'Of course the wedding won't be for ages and ages, not until I've passed my exams and got my degree and maybe worked for a bit. But it's lovely being in love and yet when I saw Toby for the first time I didn't even like him.'"

"Toby?" Nancy wondered. "It *can't*

be Toby Soames, the Rector's son. He's only a poor curate and Candy always wanted to be rich."

"'How do you think I'll fit in as a church wife, big sister? I was never really an atheist at all; Toby saw it for a pose, which was quite true. We see each other about twice a month and it's all so wonderful, I wish you could be in love, too.'"

"There must be something about the air of Greendales," Nancy told Don as they both arrived home together soaking one very wet day. "Candida is engaged to Toby Soames. I've just seen the Rector and he and his wife are delighted."

"Toby's a good lad with a rapier-keen mind. He and your sister should be very happy because she's an intelligent girl despite her butterfly displays of insouciance and apparent disregard for other people's feelings. Why don't we go out for a game of darts and a drink tonight? Let's celebrate this engagement."

"Do you feel like celebrating?"

"Well, we can't hide away for ever. I'll pick you up at seven and we'll eat a snack at the Dog and Duck."

Nancy tried to believe that Don was a little happier that evening. He certainly enjoyed their darts game, with Nancy hitting almost anything but the board which had the pub in an uproar of hilarity.

"Better than sitting at home wallowing in depression," said Don, as they ate warm steak pies and drank welcome light ale together. "We must do this again."

Nancy would not have been sitting home wallowing in depression on her own account, but on Don's, and she was glad he had been able to laugh again, for laughter, she knew, is a very healing thing when the soul has been in pain.

Some days ago she had finally written Barry, telling him exactly what she thought of him coming to Crag Lee and luring away the lady who had used the house as her second home up till then. Barry's reply had been indignant.

"Lured her, did I?" he had asked. "She was only too eager to shake the dust of Cumbria off her dainty feet. I mentioned there might be a job at our hospital and she was all ears, and nobody was more surprised than I when she turned up for interview, and later with the business as a *fait accompli*. I don't deny that we have been a little more than just friends since she came here, but she's an adult and didn't mention any ties she had with Greendales. Isn't your imagination running riot, ducky? Just because you're such a little puritan don't imagine everybody agonizes over falling in love and dreams only of wedding bells and roses round the cottage door thereafter. In other words, Nancy, grow up and accept the world as it is. This lady needed no lure. She wanted a change of venue and seized her opportunities. I object to being made to appear the villain of the piece because other people think I'm a nice sort of fellow, whereas you couldn't be shot of me fast enough."

Don was due for a week's leave and told Nancy he would spend it with his parents in Lincolnshire. "I haven't visited the old dears for such ages," he told Nancy, who was feeling a heaviness in the pit of her stomach at the news, "so I shall salve my conscience at the same time."

An elderly man, Doctor Wisley, came out of retirement to fill the gap. He was still remarkably agile, mentally, and had kept up to date with his medicine. He was a Lancastrian and called Nancy 'nobbut a lass' and was inclined to pat her on the head rather than listen to her opinions when they met over coffee.

"There, there, me dear. You're young and you'll learn. No matter how many new drugs they discover in their laboratories to cure things, it's the doctor's early assessment which is invaluable. When you've seen patients as long as I have you can pick out the shams from the sick a mile off. Just look at their eyes and the colour of 'em. You never saw a rosy-cheeked corpse, did you?"

At times Nancy wondered what her temporary colleague was talking about but never argued. It was only for a week after all. Only for a week — !

She sat looking at the empty chair opposite hers listlessly over dinner one evening. Mrs Waddell had made tasty rissoles but the second one stuck in Nancy's throat.

"Here! here!" said the housekeeper, pouting her magnificent bosom warningly. "We're not slimming, are we? Or — or suffering from this anor — anor — whatever it is?"

"*Anorexia nervosa?*" Nancy supplied with a small smile. "No. Nothing like that I'm just not hungry."

"You're missing that young man of yours if you ask me, Doctor."

Nancy had to think before she replied.

"You mean I'm off my food because of Dr Humphries?"

"I know all the signs. I once went off mine when I was nineteen and a young man from the cricket eleven let me down. That was before I met Mr Waddell. *He* never gave me cause to fret."

"Well, I'm not fretting for Dr Humphries, I can assure you. I scarcely give him a thought. Perhaps I could manage a little of the peach flan and a cup of coffee. Then I'll clear up, Mrs Waddell, so you can go."

"Right, Doctor. I must say you always leave my kitchen very tidy. So there you are and I'll say goodnight."

"Goodnight, Mrs Waddell."

The opposite chair looked emptier than ever and the portion of peach flan eventually disappeared down the waste-disposal unit.

"I'll look up a job when I've cleared up," Nancy told herself. "I'm staring a great big hiatus in the face at the moment and that's not good."

With a record of Brahms in the background Nancy looked down the column of job vacancies and sighed.

"I suppose I'd better go back to a city. I may not be as lucky in another rural backwater as I've been here, and it was such tough going at first being a woman."

She wrote a letter to an agency in Leeds which promised to place locums for a consideration, where they were needed. She added the information that she wanted to live in, enclosed a history sheet and put the letter on the hall-table for posting.

How empty the house felt, and she now noticed for the first time that the flat over the surgery was unoccupied. When Don was in residence there were always sounds, soft music, or the muted roar of a crowd's shouting as he watched a rugby match on TV or some other such thing. God! How she missed him. It was awful. He was probably enjoying a game of chess with his father or strolling down to the local pub with him for a drink, or allowing his mother to parade family photographs in front of him, simple domestic things which she, personally, would never be able to do again. She had piped a self-pitying tear before she could help it and then she walked over to the television set and switched it on. The programme was a political debate; one of the speakers had a badly fitting toupee and another certainly neither knew nor cared how to knot his crumpled tie or fasten his jacket. When Nancy realized she was criticizing the debaters rather than listening to their words she switched the set off quickly and picked up her current library book instead with a long, deep sigh.

★ ★ ★

Mrs Waddell looked set to stay with two coffees on a tray and a mound of her home-made crumbly biscuits.

"The old man's gone out to do his visiting," she announced. "He had the baby clinic this afternoon."

"I do hope it's not all too much for him at his age," Nancy said with a little frown. "How would he take it if I offered to do the clinic?"

"Oh, don't you dare, Doctor. He likes feeling important again and he'll make old bones will Dr Wisley. You're getting nice big surgeries again, aren't you? The people here have grown to trust and like you. We'll miss you, you know, when you've gone."

"Well, thanks, Mrs Waddell, but it will be nice for you having Doctor and Mrs Gray back."

"Yes. They're part of the scenery, so to speak. Whatever will you do, Doctor?"

"How do you mean?"

"Well, is it easy to get another post? I read somewhere we're turning out too many doctors and they can't get jobs, not all of them."

"Oh, I'll manage something, I think. Don't worry about me."

"Well, it's getting nearer, isn't it? A

matter of a few weeks? I was talking to my Norman last night about you, saying I wouldn't like to just get nicely settled somewhere and then have to pack up and move on. I — "

"Mrs Waddell, you shouldn't bother your husband with my concern, or yourself, come to that. It's really nobody's business but mine — "

Clatter! went Mrs Waddell's coffee cup into her saucer.

"Well, I'm sorry, Doctor, I'm sure. I won't intrude on you any more. I came for a friendly chat, not to be as good as told to shut up."

"Mrs Waddell!" Nancy said in desperation to the departing erect figure and shapely legs. "Please come back. I didn't mean to hurt your feelings. I — I'm not well."

"Why didn't you say so?"

Nancy managed a sniff or two.

"I could have flu coming on and that makes me short tempered. I actually snapped at two patients this morning and that won't do at all."

"I shall make you a hot toddy tonight. Have another biscuit. You should feed a cold."

Nancy half smiled as she heard this old wives' tale fed to her literally in crumbly biscuits.

"Oh, I'll live. And really don't worry about me, though it's sweet of you to do so. I wrote last night to an agency which places doctors like me in jobs which is the way I got this one. Doctors are always falling ill or going on holiday and needing locums. It isn't as though I'm a student looking for her first job. I have a good bit of experience behind me now. I've certainly added to it here. It's a real general practice."

"And people have cause to remember you."

"Oh! I only did my job."

"You did special things. What about that bone you took out of Johnny Spence's throat, for instance? I'll bet he remembers you. You were that kind and reassuring even when you had to hurt him. And what about going down that hole after young Timmy Bates? I heard from one of the police, who lives near me, how you just stripped off your clothes and wriggled through that crack like a worm, and how you were all bloody and bruised and dog-bitten when they got you back. It would make you blush what Constable Lott said about you. There's no doubt in my mind that you'll be missed and talked about for years to come."

"Well, I haven't gone yet and now *I'd* better go and do some visiting. You're bad for me, Mrs Waddell. We get chatting and I lose all count of time. Thanks for the coffee and biscuits."

"Now wrap up that cold. My mother always said one should wear something across the chest, a scarf or a shawl or — best of all — a piece of red flannel — "

"Mrs Waddell! You're making me laugh so I can't be so bad. See you later."

Nancy didn't do much laughing

that week, however. The days dragged heavy-footedly and the evenings were endless. There were even less night calls than usual and often she would awaken at three in the morning and be unable to get off to sleep again. Once she crept downstairs to make herself a hot milk drink. It was raining and a wind was soughing round the eaves. February was busily filling dykes and at that hour even the kitchen was cold with the fire gone out in the range and the boiler switched off. Nancy trailed back to bed and was amazed when she felt her shoulder being shaken and Mrs Waddell gazing into her surprised countenance.

"Your tea, Doctor. You slept in. Surgery in half an hour so you have a cuppa and then a quick shower."

"Is it really that time? I must — "

"*Drink your tea!*" commanded her mentor. "Now I don't allow my doctors to miss their refreshments. Be a good girl, now."

Pansy Hulme was having bigger and bigger doses of relieving morphine and Lily was becoming a nuisance during Nancy's many visits to the Grange.

"What're you doing here again, eh?" she demanded as Nancy trailed up to the front door, carrying her bag. "Are you going to hurt Panthy?"

"I don't hurt her, Lily. I make her pain better. Let me go in, please."

"Only if you'll play chathe-me-round-the-garden when you come back out."

"I can't play because I'm busy today. I'm not only busy seeing Pansy but I have to see old Mrs Haskins and Mr Watkin and Mrs Jacques. Now let me in and don't be stupid."

Lily's little eyes looked red and vicious in her puffy face and she stepped away from the front door. Mrs Jenkins waylaid Nancy in the hall.

"That Lily's getting beyond me, Doctor. I can't do a thing with her

at times and that poor thing — "
she nodded upstairs — "can't help
any more. She's got to be taken away
and put in Burford Lodge, Doctor.
You must get Pansy to agree for all
our sakes."

"I'll do my best, Mrs Jenkins."

Pansy Hulme's eyes were greedy for
the relieving needle.

"There, Miss Hulme."

"Good! I shall get up for tea when
I feel a little stronger."

"Don't you think you'd be better in
hospital?"

"But Lily — "

"Yes. I want to talk to you about
Lily. It's really the kindest thing to
send her away. You shouldn't have to
worry about Lily as you are."

There was a long, uneasy silence.

"I *have* been thinking things out,
Doctor, and please don't think I'm
angry with you as I used to be. I
was always more angry at fate than
you. I knew I was ill but refused to
acknowledge it until you made me. I

was often very rude and unco-operative with you, but you have been so kind and attentive and good with Lily that I am really most grateful. I now agree that Lily should go away. You can make the arrangements. There's just one thing I'd like you to do for me to make it easier."

"I'll do anything I can, Miss Hulme."

"Well, the people from Burford usually collect their patients in a sort of ambulance with bars on the windows. I used to threaten Lily with that when she was much younger and being awkward. 'They'll take you away in the prison wagon,' I would say, and she'd cry and throw herself round my legs and promise to be good. I know she'll have remembered and start to scream the minute they come for her. Doctor, I wondered if you could take Lily to Burford, in your car? She loves car rides. You could pack a picnic. They do say Burford Lodge is lovely nowadays, and I'm sure Lily would soon — soon settle down with the others. Oh, Doctor!"

Nancy took the thin figure into her arms.

"Very well, Miss Hulme, I'll do as you ask. I'll have to make the arrangements, of course, and we'll need your signature on the papers together with Dr Wayne's and my own. I'll get things moving, however, so don't worry any more. You're doing the right thing. Now try to get some sleep."

* * *

Once more Nancy was regarding the empty chair opposite her own as she sipped a cup of bouillon while awaiting the main course at dinner but her thoughts were on how to handle the Lily Hulme situation. She was toying with the idea of sedating Lily lightly before their journey, not so that she was not too sleepy to enjoy their carride but just to subdue the woman's

221

ebullience. Lily was like a St Bernard dog puppy, big enough to knock most other breeds of puppy flying when she only intended to play. A tablet mixed with a packet of dolly-mixtures would, no doubt, just settle her down physically without affecting her mental stimulus. It was worth a try anyway, for an excited Lily bouncing about in a car was enough to cause an accident.

After dinner, when she was alone, Mrs Waddell having gone home, the front door bell suddenly shrilled, making her jump.

The door in a doctor's house was always opened when required, though Nancy had put it on a restraining chain. She now peered through the aperture, not seeing anyone for a moment, then Don appeared with a suitcase in each hand. He waved to a disappearing taxi.

"Don!" Nancy couldn't restrain herself. "You're back! I wasn't expecting you until tomorrow."

She unhooked the chain and threw herself upon him, raining kisses of welcome upon his cheeks and finally on his lips.

"Nancy?"

"Yes, Don?"

"Just a moment. I'll put my cases down, go out again and come back. Don't go away."

This time he came through the door arms extended and she hurled herself into them and was crushed to his chest in a long, satisfying embrace.

They looked at each other, eventually, and Nancy lowered her eyes under their dark lashes a bit shyly.

"Sorry, Don! I forgot myself."

"I hope not. I was just hoping you'd discovered yourself."

"What does that mean?"

"Well, I rather hoped to be there when you did. Nancy emerging from the chrysalis of her past into the full flight of her future. Nancy, I'm trying to say I love you. What were you saying when I arrived?"

"I hadn't got as far as words, but I've been so miserable and lonely without you, Don. I suppose I must have loved you a long time. What *are* we saying? Can it all be true?"

# 10

NANCY rustled up a meal for the new arrival, watched him eat with the greatest of pleasure, gave him a slice of jam tart with cream, finally made coffee for two and thankfully sat down beside him on the capacious sofa. He pulled her close to him, saying he could manage his coffee with one hand, and she felt his warmth and his closeness and the grip of his fingers on her waist with a shrilling of every nerve in her body.

"Now where were we?" he asked finally. "Or, more important, where are we going from here, my love?"

"Do you really mean that, Don? Am I your love?"

"Almost from the first moment of our meeting, which I seem to remember was not exactly an auspicious occasion. You hit me somewhere in the solar plexus and I never quite recovered after that. Privately I was thinking 'Damn the woman! How dare she talk to me like that?' But my heart was doing a samba in my chest and that hadn't happened to me in a long, long time. I was contentedly heading towards bachelordom and you make me think I was missing out on life. Offering nothing, yet taking everything away I thought I had."

"But what about Myra? She was here a lot and we — Mrs Waddell and I — thought you were patching things up."

"I was being nice to Myra but all else was over and done with, so far as I was concerned. Myra needed attention from the opposite sex, but I still wonder if she knows the meaning of the word love. She is sadly repressed emotionally. Maybe your Barry will be good for her. Now that business was a bad time for me, coming upon you and he in a clinch — "

"I'm glad you called it that, which

was exactly what it was. It was Barry calling that particular tune and a girl can't even protest with no breath left in her lungs. I told Barry in no uncertain terms to stop that sort of thing with me. After a while he got the message. We've been barking up quite a few wrong trees, haven't we? Oh, Don, I wonder if I'm repressed?"

"Shall we see?" he asked softly. He reached out an arm and put the lamp out above the sofa. There was a long, meaningful silence and then two deep sighs.

"Not a bit," Don said unsteadily. "I would say you're a miniature volcano. May I — ?" he undid the two buttons at the top of her blouse and placed his lips near her heart, which was thudding like his own.

"We have to talk," he said at last. "We have to talk about a wedding. Have you any objections to weddings?"

"None that I can think of, provided you mean our wedding."

"I do." He put the lamp back on.

"It's got to be fairly soon. I liked you just a little too much for a moment there and I instinctively know you would want to be married."

"Is that ridiculously old-fashioned of me?"

"Of course, of both of us. I feel the same." All in a moment they were kissing and hugging and laughing like two children.

"Oh, Don!"

"Likewise, oh, Nancy!"

"Actually, it's Annette, if we're going to be married."

"Donald Leslie Arthur. Don't laugh!"

"I'm not. I'm so happy. I — "

The telephone shrilled.

"If that's Mrs Tyler with wind I'll throttle her," Don promised, as he got up. "I have to go out," he came back to say. "Old Grandpa Wilson has fractured his hip, his son thinks. Get the ambulance for me, will you, Nancy? Perkins' Cottages, Number three. I'll give the old boy a shot and see what else I can do. You realize this could happen from here on for ever in the middle of anything we're doing? Do you still want to marry me?"

"Warts and all," she told him, helping him into his warm coat. "Drive carefully."

"I'll be late, so go to bed. The next call may be for you."

She stood watching the car disappear and then sighed happily and began to tidy the kitchen.

They thought they were being so discreet, so punctitious in their behaviour that nobody would notice anything, but Mrs Waddell soon had her finger on the pulse of what was happening under what she thought of as her roof.

"Waiting for Doctor coming in then?" she asked one evening after about a week, as Nancy was obviously on tenter-hooks and watching the clock tick lugubriously in the corner. "He did say he might be late and that you were to start."

"No, I'll wait," Nancy said promptly. "I'm not ravenous."

"Well, I've done a fillet of lamb. Got some new potatoes at the shop today."

"Mm! Sounds delicious and smells even more so. Was that a car?"

"I think it was Mr Pendleton driving past. He does about this time. Really, Doctor, anybody would think you're in love!"

"They would?" Nancy was startled. "Mrs Waddell, what are you saying?"

"That you and Dr Wayne have at last seen the light, maybe? You were made for each other from the start. I didn't take any notice of any spats you had at the beginning. Things usually start between a likely couple like that. I must confess when you had a young man turn up at Christmas I was just a bit thrown and wondered if I might be wrong. But, now, well — !" and the woman beamed broadly.

"Mrs Waddell, you have absolutely no reason to suppose what you are supposing. Just because I'm waiting dinner out of common courtesy — !"

The smile became even more knowing however. "Why, it was you who told me about Sister Temple coming back into Don's — I mean Dr Wayne's — life."

"Yes. But he must have found her out for what she really is. She was only nice to him, not to me or — to you. She tried to find things out about you from me, but I didn't tell her a thing."

"What sort of things?"

"Well, whether I knew if you had a young man, or not. I said if you hadn't you should have dozens, because you were a really sweet girl. I rubbed it in, I can tell you."

"Well, thanks, Mrs Waddell. But I still don't know why you think — ?"

"I notice you're not denying it, Doctor."

"No. I'm simply not going to take any notice of what you're saying. You're guessing."

"Am I? Well, here he comes now."

Nancy promptly felt herself grow

231

scarlet up to the eyebrows.

"I'll let him in, Mrs Waddell. You serve up and then you can go. And don't go spreading gossip, now."

"As if I would, Doctor. I've been employed in this house long enough to know the meaning of discretion. You have a pleasant evening, now."

Nancy greeted Don on the doorstep with muted ecstasy.

"I had to warn you to be careful," she dimpled. "Mrs Waddell suspects. She's been very coy with me all evening though she can't be sure. When we go in to dinner remember I'm your colleague. We'll be discussing one of your cases."

"We're not going to be able to keep secrets for long from the likes of Mrs Waddell. She had been longing for me to have a grand romance ever since I arrived here. Myra was OK at first and then she began, in her inimitable way, to disapprove of our liaison. However, I have just confirmed young Mrs Arnott's pregnancy, so we can be rejoicing about that when we go in, if you like."

It was too wonderful to be truly in love to hide anything, Nancy soon discovered. Love bloomed on her usually pale cheeks so that patients remarked how well she was looking, and she replied that the air of Greendales agreed with her. She couldn't see enough of Don, or he of her. Their work kept dividing them, interfering with their romance, and yet moments spent together became the more precious by reason of their rarity. Nancy hadn't yet told Candida, and wondered if she should. She discussed matters with Don on an evening when there were sure to be no interruptions as they were both off duty together.

"I have told no one, either," Don told her, as they cuddled together on the large sofa. "It's difficult to think straight while you're tickling my ear, so be good and I'll be serious. I think the first people to be told should be Doctor and Mrs Gray, as they were responsible for bringing us together. Once they know, and approve, as I'm sure they will, we can announce our engagement and I'll buy you a ring. We can then inform our families and friends and plan a wedding as early as convenient. Do you agree to all this, my love? Can you keep your sister in the dark a week or two longer?"

"Oh, I think so. She's wrapped up in her own love affair in any case. Isn't it odd that Greendales should provide both of us with our future husbands?" She gazed at him adoringly. "Future husband," she sighed. "I still can't believe it. Twelve o'clock is going to strike at any moment and you'll turn into a pumpkin, or something."

"Oh, I'm real enough." He kissed her hungrily to prove it. "Have you thought about the future? Your career?"

Nancy's jaw dropped for an instant. "No, I haven't," she replied. "I — I suppose I'll have to drop it to — to be a real wife to you. That's my primary ambition, now."

"Well, thanks, love, for saying that and meaning it. I couldn't hold you to it, however, knowing what a grand little doctor you are and how you'd miss doing your job after a while. There may be no need for you to drop it, as you suggest."

"But what alternative is there? I have no intention hieing me off to some dingy practice in Leeds, leaving my husband here in Greendales. I have some ambition, but not at the expense of our happiness."

"Bless you for that, sweetheart! I have no intention of sending you packing, either. Before the old doctor went off to Australia he and I had a serious chat. He asked me how I'd like to take over the practice and hire an assistant to help me. He believes his seizure was a warning to take things more easily in future. Mrs Gray was also quite adamant that she had no ambitions to become a widow. At the time I wasn't too sure I wanted to settle down, here, so I said we'd discuss matters when he got back. But now I may have just the 'assistant' I've always been looking for and Greendales suddenly seems a very pleasant place to me."

Nancy squealed in excitement, "Oh, Don, it all sounds too good to be true. I'd love to be your assistant and your wife. Where would we live?"

"If all goes as I plan we'd squeeze into the flat until I could buy us a house. It may even be that the Grays won't want to keep this rambling place on with their daughter so far away. Would you object to being mistress of Crag Lee?"

"Not at all. I suppose if we're both working we keep Mrs Waddell on? After all, she thinks of it as her house, too."

"Plans are all in the future, pet. These matters are crosses on t's and dots on i's. The meat is that we have each other till death us do part."

"I'll settle for that, Dr Wayne. Oh! how I love you!"

It was quite late before Nancy at last

remembered something.

"Oh, Don, before you g — "

"Yes, my sweet?"

"I want you to sign some papers. I've got Lily Hulme into Burford Lodge and I'm taking her, personally, tomorrow, pretending we're going out for a drive and a picnic. That's the way Pansy wants it so her little sister, as she thinks of her, won't be upset by the ambulance they use. Pansy really can't hang on any longer. She must go back into hospital as soon as Lily has gone. Those two have been the most distressing elements of my work here. I try to be merely objective but I feel for Pansy, trying not to admit she's ill, for Lily's sake, and even for Lily, a little girl trapped in a healthy woman's body. I do hope she'll settle down at Burford."

"It's a very good institution and Lily will have companions. I know Dr Gray used to argue with Pansy by the hour. He'll be glad the deed is done, though he'll be sorry to hear the elder Hulme sister was so ill for so long. Now there are your papers. Are you sure you wouldn't like me to go along?"

"No, thanks. I'm going to slip Lily a Valium. She's cute, you know, and if there were two of us she might smell a rat. As it is, she was happily telling old Mrs Jennings what she wanted for her picnic when last I saw her. Our trip happens to coincide with her birthday week and tomorrow's jaunt is her treat. Poor old Lily! Some treat."

"Now continue to be objective, Nancy. It's the best solution all round and you know it. She could live another thirty years."

"Right! I'll let you go off to bed, now, darling. I won't see you for lunch but we'll have dinner together as usual, eh?"

"Wouldn't miss it for worlds." Another coming together, a long sigh and then the closing of the door between them.

When Nancy remembered their earlier conversation she felt so happy she could have sung. Simply being in love was wonderful but for life suddenly to have such possibilities was fantastic. To be happily married and working in harness with one's beloved spouse in a job they both loved! How strange were the workings of fate! She had come here very much a stranger in a strange land, a woman doctor, no less, in territory where men had lorded it for generations. She could still remember the row of almost empty chairs at her first surgeries, now seeming so long ago, and how hard it had been to become accepted in every sense.

"Oh! I could mull over it for hours but I must get some sleep," she now decided. "I have a busy day, tomorrow, one way and another."

* * *

Lily was dressed in a floral frock which was obviously one of her favourites; her iron-grey hair bounced where curlers had been removed. She wore a necklace of coral beads round her thick neck, almost hidden by her double chin, and she was dancing in her excitement.

"I'm going in the car! I'm going in the car!" she sang. "How thuper!"

Pansy had managed to dress and was downstairs, finding difficulty in standing upright.

"Now, you're to be good, Lily," she said wearily. "Don't be a nuisance to Doctor."

"I'm not a nuithanthe. Am I?" Lily asked, trying to sound plaintive.

"No. Don't get too excited," Nancy advised. "You and Mrs Jennings pack the picnic and I'll just have a word with Pansy."

She proceeded to give the elder sister a relieving injection. "They should soon be here for you, Miss Hulme. Don't worry about Lily. I'll come to see you in hospital as soon as I can. Now I'd better go or your ambulance will be arriving. Good luck!"

Lily was bouncing in the passenger seat.

"Where are we having our picnic, Doctor?"

"I thought in the woods. I'm taking you to see the deer in Holtam Park. We have to keep very still or we might frighten them away."

"Have you got any toffeeth?"

"Of course. Would I forget those? Here you are."

Lily chewed dolly-mixtures happily as the car drove off through the lanes.

"Ooh! That'th a hard one." She examined the tablet of Valium critically.

"Swallow it," said Nancy. "It's quite small and will slip down."

"No." Lily was adamant. "I don't like hard oneth. Throw it away. Nathty."

Nancy saw the Valium tablet sail out through the portion of open window and sighed. Lily may not be normal for her age but she was no fool, either. The dolly mixtures disappeared all too quickly and then she was asking, "How long before the picnic, Doctor? I'm hungry."

"How can you be, Lily? You're full of sweets."

"But I've seen treeth and thingth before. I want our picnic and to see the deer." She bounced in her seat.

"Be still, Lily. I have to drive carefully down these narrow lanes. Leave your seat-belt alone."

"I don't like it. It holdth me in."

"That's what it's meant to do. Now you've loosened it. If you're going to be naughty we're going home and no picnic."

"No. I'll be good. I'll thit thtill."

They still had about ten miles to go to Holtam Park, where Nancy proposed they picnic, and then Burford Lodge was a mere two miles distant.

"Ooh! A bird. A very big bird in that tree!" Lily leaned over Nancy to point.

"Sit back, Lily. It was probably a heron. Somebody round here has a pair comes every year. Are you enjoying yourself?"

"Mm — mm. I'm thtill hungry. Hurry up and thtop."

"You look out for birds and squirrels

on your side. Tell me what you see but don't knock my arm."

After five minutes came a plaintive voice. "I want to — you know? I forgot to go. Panthy didn't tell me."

"Oh, Lily, can't you wait 'til we stop?"

"No. I'm nearly doing it. Thtop! Thtop!"

"I can't stop in the middle of a lane on a bend. Just wait ten seconds."

"You're to thtop now, do you hear? I'll do it in your car."

Lily grabbed hold of the wheel and pulled. Nancy couldn't believe it. This silly woman was going to cause them to have an accident before they could enjoy the promised picnic if she wasn't careful. It had been a mistake to undertake to take Lily into her charge. She was too unpredictable.

Nancy managed to get Lily's hand off the wheel but the passenger door suddenly shot open and Nancy had a horrified vision of Lily falling out before she found herself careering into a small field on her left, crashing through a fence and hurtling through space as the ground dropped under the wheels of the car. She had no time to do anything but unfasten her own seat-belt, wondering all the time about Lily whose screams were rending the air somewhere above her. The open car door hit a tree, made it swing round and Nancy hurtled through the windscreen like a toy doll. She didn't know she had broken her leg and an arm, she didn't know a thing as she lay in a gathering pool of blood, for she had lost consciousness. A van driver and his mate saw a demented-looking woman dancing in their path.

"Oh, God!" said Bert. "It's one o' them loonies from the home. She must 'ave escaped."

"There's a car down there," said Jack, "and what looks like a bundle of rags. Oh, my lord, it must be the driver. There's blood everywhere. Better see what we can do, Bert. There's a telephone up ahead. You

phone the home to tell them about
the fat one and say the other looks
dead an' what about it? I'll go take
a look-see. Wish I'd done first aid,
now."

# 11

DON looked down at his beloved, plastered and bandaged and attached to a drip and sighed deeply with love and pain. This was the third day after the accident and so far she hadn't opened her eyes to him. He was consumed with guilt that he, who knew Lily Hulme so much better than this darling did, had allowed her to take full responsibility for conveying the child-woman to the special hospice for the afflicted. Nancy had made a promise to a dying woman, however, and Nancy would have taken some persuading to break such a promise.

At the hospital, which was Myra's old stamping-ground, they had told him the patient's condition was now stable and she was not in danger; they went so far as to say that she had come off remarkably lightly. The fractures she had sustained were not compound, and she had instinctively covered her face with her arms as she shot through the windscreen so that most of her stitches were in these members. But she had been unconscious for forty-eight hours and a dark bruise over her left temple showed that she had taken a heavy blow in that area. Again good news, however, no skull fracture and she had apparently regained consciousness during the night and asked quite brightly what on earth she was doing in a hospital, joking that she was more used to working in one than taking it easy.

"You're not taking it so easy, Doctor," the night sister had said. "You had a nasty accident and you have to be mended just like anybody else."

"An accident? — ?" Nancy had looked vague, winced as she tried to lift her arm.

"Yes, my dear. Now you're due for your pain-relievers and I want you to sleep. Be a good girl, now."

All this had been related to Don

when he had arrived, having again had to call Dr Wisley to relieve him, and he badly wanted to hear Nancy's voice for himself.

She was sleeping like the Princess Beauty, however, as though she could go on for a hundred years. He couldn't stay all day as he would have wished to; he had to do boring things like filling in an insurance claims form for Dr Gray's car, a complete write-off, and await the assessor's visit; he had also written the department on Nancy's behalf, which dealt with doctors' accidents while about their lawful duties. There was all the paperwork and the patients and his aching heart which stayed on here long after he had to leave. Candida, whom he had informed of the accident, had rushed north and spent the morning with her sister.

"But she just sleeps," Candida had reported. "They say she'll be OK in time, however."

"Oh, yes," Don had assured her. "Fractures heal and your sister normally enjoys very good health. Shock accounts for the fact that she's sleeping a lot at the moment. That can only do her good."

Candida was coming back this evening, and after a night's sleep at the house had to return to Oxford as this was the year of her final examinations. It would do Nancy no good if she hung about Greendales and risked missing lectures which were important to her career.

Don was having trouble with his eyes. They were watering as though he had a cold coming on. He would never admit to crying. Men didn't cry.

He replaced his handkerchief in his pocket and behold a quizzical pair of brown eyes regarding him from the bed.

"Nancy?" he said with a quick smile. "Hello, darling, it's me!"

"I can see that, Don. How are you?"

"How am I, she asks! You're the invalid, pet. How are *you*? Any pain?"

"Not at the moment. Who's looking after our patients?"

"Old Wisley, so don't worry." He took her uninjured hand and kissed it. "God! Nancy, but you had me worried."

"They tell me I had an accident. Was the car badly damaged?"

"Worse than you. But cars are things and can be replaced. You're my concern."

He wanted badly to kiss her on the lips but was afraid of hurting her. She looked so little, somehow, so girlish with a pucker of a frown between her brows.

"I don't remember the accident, Don. Not a thing. What was I doing? I'm normally a very careful driver."

"I suppose you were being careful but you had Lily Hulme in the car. Nobody saw what she did but there's no doubt she caused you to lose control. Anyway, she's safely in Burford Lodge, now, and I've let her sister know without telling her

250

the rest, which would only upset her."

"Oh! So Pansy finally agreed to let Lily go, did she? That's a relief. I must have bumped my head. I've got quite a headache. I wonder if they could give me something for it?"

"I'll ring for the nurse, my darling."

"Don! Don't talk like that in front of her. You'll have people thinking things."

"And why shouldn't they, if they want to?"

"Because it could become embarrassing for you. Everybody here knows about you and Myra."

He looked puzzled as the Nurse arrived and gave Nancy two tablets for her headache.

"Don't visit for too long, Dr Wayne," the nurse advised. "This girl gets tired very easily."

"I won't be here much longer, Nurse." As the door closed on the blue-dressed figure he regarded the figure in the bed speculatively.

"Nancy, what's the last thing you do remember, without making your head ache worse?"

"Well, you were away on your leave, and I had just been having a chat with old Wisley about a case of Down's Syndrome, on which he has very old-fashioned views. I was surprised when I opened my eyes and saw you were back. How long have you been back?"

He felt a hollow like a wound in the centre of his chest. She didn't remember what they had been to each other, how he still felt about her. His endearments had embarrassed her. She must think he was demonstrating an outsize bedside manner.

"Not long," he answered, not wishing to worry her. "Candy's coming in later, when you've had another sleep."

"Oh! I hope she hasn't been too worried about me?"

"Well, they tell us there's not too much to worry about, actually. It's just a question of time. We all want you fit as soon as possible."

"I shall soon get sick of being in hospital. A fine one I am to act as a locum and become a liability, instead."

"We'll have you back at Crag Lee to convalesce. Nobody can help having accidents. If they could all be foreseen half our hospital wards would be empty."

"Don, I'm still very sorry about the Barry-Myra affair. They don't know, here, about her reasons for leaving, only that she said she was going to a better job. Can you ever forgive me for messing up your life?"

"Oh, Nancy, you didn't. If a woman wants to go she'll go. It wouldn't have made me any happier keeping her here against her will. Anyhow, we'd decided to split up before Barry came. You had nothing to do with it."

"You're just saying that to make me feel better."

"No. It's the truth. I'm not fretting over Myra. Now I think you'd better go back to sleep and I'll just have a word with your doctor on my way out. Goodbye for now, Nancy. Don't worry about a thing."

"I'm glad about Lily Hulme, though. She was a menace."

"You can say that again," Don added *sotto voce* as he left the room.

"Dr Devine's suffering some amnesia," he told the physician on the case.

"I was afraid of that. She took quite a crack on the head. Have you gathered how much is missing?"

"Only the whole of our brief love affair," Don wanted to say. Instead he said calmly, "About ten days. I suppose as she comes out of the trauma it could all come back."

"Some remember, some don't." Dr Dwyer said with a shrug. "Still, ten days isn't much. It might be better if she never remembers the accident. Remembering the event might shake her up all over again."

Don thought how little the man really knew what he was saying. In fact nobody else knew the story of Don and

Nancy and their love affair, not even Nancy, herself, as things were. She *had* to remember! He willed her to. Life loomed grey and featureless without her dancing-eyed welcomes and her warm little body stirring fires of desire deep within him. It was he who had decided they should not broadcast the news of their romance. Dr and Mrs Gray were to be the first to know, he remembered telling her as she lay in his arms. Well, there was no one to explain the situation to, at least, now that it was changed. His thoughts must be of Nancy's welfare, of getting her fit and strong and mobile again and hoping she would suddenly remember the good bits of those ten lost days which — he hoped — would more than make up for the bad.

It was a grim drive back to Greendales and it was raining. He could hardly bear to tell Mrs Waddell that Dr Devine had been awake and talking to him. He didn't mention the amnesia. The good woman wanted to stuff him with cakes and tea and he had to make an effort to appear normal.

Life must go on. How many times had he said that very thing to other people in his time!

★ ★ ★

The Grays had been back in residence a couple of weeks and Nancy was recuperating well and ambling about with the aid of two sticks. At first, on her discharge from hospital, she had resisted being taken in by the good doctor and his wife, but they insisted they would not hear of her going elsewhere.

"The whole village would be up in arms," quoth Mrs Gray. "You have proved to be very popular, my dear, and everybody asks about you all the time. You're staying here until you're well and strong and I want to hear no arguments."

"But I'm not pulling my weight — "

"You have done, more than your

weight. We heard about what you did at Christmas, rescuing young Tim Bates from what could well have been a grave. Nobody else but another child could have wriggled down that hole, and a child wouldn't have known what to do. *We owe you*, my dear girl. And I did say no arguments. This is your home for as long as you need one and my husband and I may have a proposition to put to you when you're really fit. I don't want to say any more about that just yet. How's the leg?"

"Aches a bit but I'm getting the muscle back. I don't enjoy walking but I realize it's the best exercise for my own rehabilitation. Another two weeks should see me back to normal."

"Oh, give it a bit longer than that. Ah! here's Don back. Now we can have lunch."

Nancy looked at Don, who smiled at her in the way he had of asking a question with his eyes. She never quite knew what the question was but thought it was about her physical progress.

"I walked as far as Pond Cottage," she told him, "and had a cup of coffee with old Mrs Carpenter."

"Well done!" he applauded her. "It's all good news lately, isn't it?"

She remembered the loneliness she had felt when he had gone away on his week's leave, how she had sat at this very table just gazing at his empty chair. Now he always seemed just a little bit cagey in her company, and she wondered if he still nourished some resentment that she had been responsible for sending Myra out of his life, no matter how he had tried to reassure her on that subject while she had been in hospital.

During lunch he said, "I'm afraid poor Pansy Hulme passed peacefully away during the night. It was the only tolerable end for her."

"Poor Pansy!" Nancy said. "did she miss seeing me at the hospital? I promised her I'd go."

"I've been in your stead," said Don, "as has Dr Gray. She was very glad to see him, wasn't she, sir? She was told you had had an accident, but we didn't tell her Lily was probably responsible."

"I can't remember what happened," Nancy frowned, passing a hand over her eyes, "but at least Lily's safe. Will they tell her the news?"

"Oh, yes. The Matron will tell her and be most kind. Lily has a friend, now, similarly afflicted. I believe they keep each other company day long."

"Oh, I'm glad!" said Nancy. "Lily needed a companion. She had me playing hide-and-seek, chase-me-round-the-garden, I don't know what, 'Agh!"

"What's the matter, dear?" Mrs Gray asked in concern. "You've gone quite pale."

"A — a pain in my head, and a sort of vision. I think it was of Lily in a floral frock and she was falling. It's gone, now. I'm all right."

"No more pain?" asked Dr Gray.

"No. I think what I need is work, sir, to take my mind off things. May I sit in with you during surgery this evening?"

"Why not? You can fill in the treatment cards. That would be a great help."

Nancy saw Don looking at her oddly. "I'm all right, really," she told him. "Another week and I'll challenge you to a return darts match at the Dog and Duck. This time I may even hit the board."

"Done!" said Don with a crooked little smile. "I shall look forward to that."

Candida Devine was visiting her beloved in Leeds. Toby worked in a poor parish but it was always heavenly walking with him through the rundown streets. She squeezed the arm threaded through her own and exclaimed, "Thank heavens the exams are over! I should be OK but, naturally, I do have periods of self-doubt. I'll stay on until the results are through and then

I'd better park myself in Greendales once more. I worry about Nancy."

"But I thought she was doing so well — ?"

"Oh, she is. She walks with just one stick, now, and is taking some of the surgeries, but there's something niggles me."

"What is it, my darling?"

"This loss of memory business."

"But it's only a matter of ten short days, Candy, not half a lifetime. She hasn't forgotten how to do her job or anything important."

"How do we know, Toby? Would you like to lose rememberance of even one week of your life? Wouldn't you wonder what had happened during that week?"

"Surely somebody could tell her? She knows she had an accident, for one thing."

"Yes, but she can't remember it for herself. Being told by another person is like reading it in a book. It didn't happen to her but to this other character. If I lost my memory and you said, 'Candy, I don't love you any more. It happened while you were suffering from amnesia,' I know I'd get a terrible shock but I'd wonder if It was true. I don't suppose I'd really believe it though I'd worry about it."

"Well, I'm not likely to tell you that, my love, amnesia or no amnesia. I love you very much and it's likely to go on with me for life."

"Oh, Toby, bless you for that! I want to get married tomorrow when you say such sweet things to me. I'm getting all the bouquets and Nancy is getting the kicks. That's the story of our lives, I'm afraid."

"Nancy never had a serious romance, then?"

"Not to my knowledge. There was Barry, of course, but she told me she couldn't go on with him. She was quite heart-free at Christmas. Naturally, I want everybody to be in love because we are. I would have thought Don Wayne and she might have hit it off, but nothing seems to have developed in that direction, worse luck! So she's never going to meet anybody in Greendales, is she? That brings me to another point I want to discuss with you."

"Fire ahead!"

"Nancy's itching to work full-time again. She thinks the Grays have shewn her hospitality long enough. Apparently Dr Gray has offered to make her his assistant so that he can gradually retire. That means Don will take over the main practice and Nancy would work under him. She'd practically be stuck there for life."

"Would that be so bad? Greendales is my home, remember."

"But you *have* left it to make your own way, my dear. You couldn't have been happy as a curate in Greendales, could you?"

"You might have a point there, darling."

"So I don't want Nancy stuck away, never meeting anybody but the locals. In any case, she has an offer of a residential post here in Leeds — obviously she applied because she thought she'd be near us, before her accident — and here she'd meet lots of people, maybe some nice man, and — what are you laughing at? I've told you I want my sister to have a shot at married life, not dry up into a lemon of a spinster. I know she's torn, wondering what to decide, and I shall urge her to come to Leeds."

"Do you really think she needs help in coming to a decision? Your sister struck me as a young woman quite capable of running her own life."

"But you haven't seen her since the accident, have you? She had changed mentally, grown broody. She goes off into brown studies and when I talked to her seriously one day she says she gets depressed easily and has regular nightmares. I think she needs to get right away from that particular scene."

"Well, you can paint the picture for her, and assure her we'd love to have her near us, but don't be dictatorial."

"Do you find me dictatorial?"

"No. Your concern for Nancy does you credit. When I first knew you I thought you a selfish brat. No! Don't hit me! Not here in the street. I have friends who would rough you up for less."

The couple went off laughing into the distance, hand in hand, and Nancy Devine, the subject of their conversation, was suffering one of her depressions in the sitting-room of Crag Lee. It was not often Mrs Waddell found the young doctor alone these days, with her employers back in residence, but Dr and Mrs Gray had gone out to dine at the Rectory. Nancy was covering the telephone but so far it had not rung.

"Ready for dinner, Doctor?" asked Mrs Waddell, chummily. "It's a bit early but I have it all ready."

"I'll have dinner by all means, Mrs Waddell. You may be able to get away a bit earlier. I must warn you I'm not very hungry."

"Well, you haven't been since your accident, have you, dear? What bit there was of you has grown less. You'd better watch you don't fall down a grid one of these days. I've done you a nice bit of veal with mushrooms. You should enjoy that. Dr Wayne's in the flat so why are you on your own?"

"I believe he's entertaining a college friend. They're going out to the pub later."

"Have you and he had a row of some sort?"

Nancy blinked.

"What makes you say that, Mrs Waddell? Why should we have had a row because he's seeing an old friend?"

"Well, I — er — I used to think — " the housekeeper had been warned that Dr Devine was not to be subjected to interrogations. She got bad headaches when she tried to think about things. "I'll get your dinner," Mrs Waddell said in some confusion, and set down a plate and a silver dish in front of

266

the lonely diner. "There! That's not too much to put you off, is it?"

"It looks lovely. But I repeat, Mrs Waddell, what made you think I had quarrelled with Dr Wayne?"

"Well, it's just that you were such good friends — "

"So we are, still. I count him as one of my best friends."

"And that's all?"

"Of course that's all. What should we be?"

"I had hoped — I really thought — oh, I'd better be off, me and my gossiping! There's a custard tart if you'd like some and a fresh jug of coffee on the hot plate. Goodnight, Doctor!"

"Goodnight, Mrs Waddell."

Nancy felt a peculiar stirring in the top of her head, which usually meant she was going to see flashing lights behind her eyes which ended in a headache. These headaches were an annoyance but didn't usually last long. She had received a bad bump in the accident, her doctors told her, and she would grow out of the trouble in time. Mrs Waddell's words had been the trigger of this present attack but she couldn't clearly remember why. Don and she never quarrelled so why should a woman think they had? Don was kindness itself, and had taken her out a couple of times to the Dog and Duck and once to dinner at the Quaker Inn. The outings had been enjoyable without being ecstatic. Nancy did not care to gush in case Don thought she was after him in some way, and his solicitude for her welfare was that of a doctor for a special patient. She read no more into it than that. She remembered him kissing her hand and calling her 'darling' when she was in hospital, but these had been expressions of relief that she was not dead or maimed for life. She remembered their friendship well enough and it had not been demonstratively emotional, except in the context of stolen kisses at Christmas and on the occasion he had taken her to a concert when Myra had been his real interest.

She didn't know what to do about Dr Gray's offer of an assistantship. It was a splendid offer in that it was to cost her nothing and she would simply work her way and be paid a small salary at first, increasing annually. The snag was that she would be working eventually under Don, and she had a feeling that Don would not always remain a bachelor. She couldn't face the idea of there being a Mrs Wayne. Don's friendship meant a lot to her but when he had a wife she would be thrown more and more to her own devices. Everything had been done to persuade her to stay on. She was to live in the flat, and Don would take a room at the Dog and Duck until other arrangements could be made.

"But I can't take over your home," she had told Don.

"Rubbish! It's not my home. I can live in a tent if necessary. You'd be very comfortable up there and I'm sure you'd want to redecorate the place. It's a bit stark for a woman. At least Myra used to say so."

She jumped as the doorbell rang while her head was still thudding.

"Don?" she questioned him in the doorway.

"Well, let me in, please," he said with a smile.

"Where's your friend?"

"Finishing his drink. I just came to see that you're OK. Not lonely?"

"No. Not lonely. It's kind of you to ask."

"I'll join you in a cup of coffee if I may?"

"Certainly. I was just going to have mine."

As she brought the cups in she blinked away the lights from behind her eyes and asked suddenly "Don, are you taking over this house, as you said?"

"Taking over this house, Nancy? It's the Grays' house."

"Silly me! I don't know what

suddenly made me think they were intending to go back to Australia to live with their daughter and you were going to buy this house. I must be dreaming, or something."

"Some dream. I'd love to take over Crag Lee in certain circumstances, but they have not arisen."

"You must think I'm mad, saying a thing like that out of the blue?"

"No. I must have transferred my dream processes to you. I have thought how grand it would be to live in this house and own the practice. Well, Nancy, thanks for the coffee. You're sure you'll be all right?"

"Of course. The Grays won't be late. They never are. Thanks again for calling."

"See you tomorrow, then."

"Don!" she called out when he had gone, and she called again rather more wildly as she felt herself falling into space. "Don! Don! Where are you, Don?"

The words were an echo. She had

spoken them on some earlier, desperate occasion. They rang round her head, now, making it ache.

"Oh, God! I've got to get away from here," she decided as reason returned a little. "I'm a doctor, and what good am I to anybody like this? I'm allowing my nerves to get the better of me. The trouble is I'm in love with that man and seeing him, bearing his consideration and kindness, is driving me round the bend."

She felt better for acknowledging her feelings for Don which had been born, she realized, while she had sat regarding his empty chair during the period of his week's leave in the early spring. There would be no getting better from such an affliction, so the best thing would be to take the Leeds appointment she had been offered and not have to see the object of her frustrated devotion every day of her life. It would be difficult telling Dr and Mrs Gray of her irrevocable decision; they had been so kind and treated her more like a daughter than a locum who had finished her appointment.by having an accident and causing a great deal of trouble all round.

"And, of course, I can't tell them why I have to refuse their offer," she pondered. "They'll think me an awful ingrate. But I'll think of something to say to soften the blow when the time comes. I wonder why I said that stupid thing to Don about his buying his house? It seemed at the time I could actually see him suggesting it, and he was very happy and laughing and full of plans. I can't have imagined it, can I? Maybe it just popped out of the lost bit of my memory and he played it down because I'm not supposed to meddle with that part of my brain. I wonder what else I forgot during those ten days? I feel I'll never rest till I know. I'm sure I dream things, because I wake up sweating and terrified, sometimes, but I can't project those terrors into my consciousness. If I could all would be solved and I'd be better equipped, with a whole memory, to decide my future and also I'd probably be shot of these damned headaches. Dr Dwyer said it needed some trigger, but trying deliberately to remember was often counter-productive and succeeded in pushing unpleasant events further back into the subconscious. The only unpleasant event I've lost is the accident itself, and there may be good things I should be remembering. I really wish I could recall the accident. I know I got hurt and I must have been terrified while it was happening, but I'd gladly go through all that again instead of the horrible limbo I feel, now, about those missing days in my life. Doctors don't know everything. They haven't all suffered from amnesia. They can't know how important it is to the sufferer to remember even one lost hour of life. It's like losing a shoe, or one earring, which makes the other useless.

I'm going to think about what Dr Dwyer said about a trigger. I don't care how many headaches I get so long as I break through that barrier in the end."

# 12

NANCY was to take afternoon tea with Don in his flat. He had suggested it that morning. "Come and really look round the place," he invited. "Mrs Waddell has offered to make home-baked crumpets and jam tarts and I make a very nice pot of tea, though I says it that shouldn't."

"I'll be delighted," she had told him, but had also decided to tell Don first of all that she had decided against staying on as assistant in the practice. He might advise her on how most delicately to broach the matter to the Grays.

She climbed the outside stairs to the flat just after the stroke of four, and Don greeted her as always, nowadays, first of all with his professional look assessing the state of her health and secondly with a glow of the eyes which was really glad to see her.

"Any pain climbing the stairs, now?" he asked, showing her into the sitting-room.

"No. All my pains are gone. My leg feels quite strong, nowadays, and the ache I had in my shoulder for so long is happily just a memory. My! But it's a long time since I was in here. I came in blazing at you with Myra in the background that first time. Do you remember? You must have had a shocking opinion of me at the time."

"I recall you were a real termagent in those days."

"Myra was most amused. I think she enjoyed seeing us at each other's throats like that. Do you hear from her, nowadays?"

"Oh, yes. Quite a regular corre-spondence." Nancy felt a sense of loss, of shock. "Nothing came of that business between her and Humphries. She can't say ill enough of him. In fact she propositioned me again, wanting to come and talk things over with me."

Nancy gulped.

"That may be nice for you," she decided. "You're obviously her best bet."

"You're joking," Don told her from the small kitchen. "I'm not here for her rebounding when other people succeed in boring her to tears. I would always listen to her, as an old friend, but there's not a chance of anything more between us. Anyhow, have you heard from Humphries?"

"Just one letter. He'd heard about my accident from somebody and wanted to know how I was, etc. I answered it and that was that."

"Now we'll have tea. Don't get up. I'll bring the trolley over there. Mrs Waddell, bless her, had done us proud. She even sent up a Victoria sandwich sponge, which she knows is my favourite cake. Can you cook, Nancy?"

"I don't know. I haven't had much experience of domesticity. I suppose one learns, but to be in the Waddell class is like being top of the tree, culinarily speaking."

"I suppose when you're living here you'll want to run your own kitchen? You may acquire a liking for cooking, and ask me to dinner sometimes."

"I would if I was staying. I wanted to talk to you about that, Don. I've been giving the matter a lot of thought and I've practically decided to leave Greendales. I wanted you to be the first to know."

"Leave Greendales?" He took a bite of crumpet and regarded her seriously. "We shall miss you, Nancy. *I* shall miss you. After resisting your appointment at the outset I've now grown used to seeing you around."

"I shall miss you, too, Don. I never had a man friend before and you have been a very good friend."

"I hope I shall continue to be. But what makes you think you should move on? Does city life call?"

"Not really. I don't think I should

279

grow roots here, that's all. I came, originally, for six months, and now I've been here nine, what with one thing and another. I can't help but feel the Grays are thinking they're responsible for me in some way. Oh! I don't know, but I'm frustrated in so many ways. I think a clean page, a move, would jolt me up in more ways than one and I'd be better for it. I'm not ungrateful but I'm not very happy at present. I don't think I'm going to be happy again until — until — "

"Yes, Nancy? Until when?"

"Until I really know what happened that day. I'm sure I'm being a complete and utter nuisance to everybody, nagging about it, and people telling me to have patience and all will be well in time, but I feel I have a gaping hole in my head and I doubt everything will come right in time if I just drift on the way I am. I feel I'm a boring person to be with, I get depressed and unsure. I even argued with Dr Gray over a diagnosis the other day and when he eventually said I could be right I wasn't sure I was. I can't be sure about anything, my mind may be playing tricks, like when I was convinced you'd mentioned buying Crag Lee and the Grays emigrating."

"No, Nancy, your mind wasn't playing tricks over that. I shouldn't have denied the possibility had crossed my mind and I mentioned it to you before the Grays came home, just before you had your accident. You see a bit of your memory did come back all of its own accord. I wish you'd wait and see if more happens before you run off and leave us. I want to be there when it does."

"But a scrap of conversation, Don, doesn't make up for ten whole days of oblivion. I've already waited a long time for a miracle to happen, but it doesn't. I know, myself, of cases of amnesia which persisted. Mine may be one of them. I dwell too much on things, here. If I get right away I'll soon have other things to think about."

"Oh, Nancy, I wish I could help you."

"I know you would if you could, Don, but you can't do my remembering for me. It's not the same. I've got quite a lot out of Mrs Waddell, one way and another, but she clams up when she realizes I'm pumping her and it doesn't do anything for me in any case."

"And what information has our dear Clementina supplied?"

For the first time Nancy smiled, momentarily looking like her old self. "Is that her name? I never knew. We're always very proper with each other. Oh, I found out more about why I was with Lily Hulme in the car when it crashed. I'd already heard that I was on my way to Burford Lodge with her, having promised Pansy I'd take her to keep her from getting frightened in the special ambulance they use. Pansy had confided in the Rector and he thought I ought to know I was on a sort of mercy mission. But Mrs Waddell told

282

me I'd promised Lily a picnic, so that she'd go with me more willingly, and that I was packing dolly mixture into my pocket when I left the house. Of course it doesn't help me to remember for myself, which is the odd thing about all this. Other people tell you what you did and it means nothing. They could have told me I'd won a medal in a race and it would mean as little unless I actually remembered winning it myself. This is a gorgeous cake, but I mustn't eat any more. What do I tell the Grays, Don, so that I don't feel and sound like a heel after all their kindness to me?"

"You're determined on leaving us, then?"

"Yes. The city practice will be much busier and that will be good for me. Eventually Candy and Toby will marry and live in Leeds, so I won't be alone."

"Well, I'd just tell them frankly, Nancy, what you've told me. They won't hold anything against you."

"Yes. I must do that. Why were you considering buying Crag Lee, Don, and thinking the old people might emigrate?"

"Well, he had mentioned the possibility of retiring when he had his seizure. Eventually he got better and changed his mind, but Mrs Gray kept on about it. What a good idea it would be, etc. I may have thought it a good idea, in those circumstances, to live over the shop, so to speak, and maybe take me a wife."

"Yes, Don. You should marry." It made her heart bleed to say it, but she wanted only his happiness. "You could do me one more favour, Don, if you would — "

"I'll help in any way I can, Nancy. What is it?"

"Well, I don't like asking the Grays, but I feel I ought to get behind the wheel of a car again. If I'm going to be working in a city I can hardly travel round on a bike. I was wondering if you'd trust me with your car?"

"Well, of course. You're a grand little driver and you can borrow my car to regain your confidence with pleasure. It will be free on Wednesday p.m. If I need one I'll take Mrs Gray's Mini Traveller. Oh, by the way, don't tell them you're leaving before Friday. Thursday is their wedding anniversary, their fortieth, I believe, and you and I are taking over while they go out and have a super meal."

"I'm glad you told me. There's just time to order some flowers. I'll collect the car on Wednesday about two-thirty, then. Don't tell anyone. I don't want people worrying about me."

"It shall be our secret. But you're not to stay out for hours now. Remember your shoulder has just stopped hurting and steering a car, after weeks of non-driving, can be tiring."

"Oh, I'll be back by four o'clock, or so. Thanks a lot, Don. As usual, it has been wonderful being with you and I enjoyed the tea."

"I'll see you down the steps."

"Oh, I'm fine, now, but thanks all the same."

She was pleasantly surprised to find that she was much less depressed after the little tea-party and felt pleasantly excited at the idea of driving a car again after so long. She was smiling as she entered the main house and encountered Mrs Waddell on her way to the kitchen.

"My, Doctor, but you do look better! More like your old self. You ought to spend more time with Dr Wayne. He's the tonic you need."

"He's certainly a pleasant fellow, Mrs Waddell, and the goodies you supplied for tea were much appreciated. Now don't expect me to eat a big dinner. I'm going for a walk, now, for the good of my health. See you later."

★ ★ ★

Sliding behind the wheel of Don's car, on Wednesday afternoon, gave her an odd feeling. Of course that was because she hadn't done such a thing since *der tag*, the day she couldn't remember, on which such terrible things had happened, including the total wreck of a perfectly good car. She never saw Dr Gray's new blue Cortina without feeling extremely self-conscious, though the insurance people had paid up to the letter.

She adjusted the seat, which allowed for Don's long legs, and put on the seat-belt, which again had to be tightened considerably, and then she wondered what she was doing there, where was she going? Tossing the sense of purposelessness aside she groped in the glove compartment for a map. It was like the one Don had given her at the beginning of her stay in Greendales, with the names of isolated houses and farms marked in in ink. That took her back. She thought she might go and see Mrs Wainwright, that middle-aged mother who had given birth to a baby girl who was her namesake; she hadn't seen mother and child since her accident and was sure of a warm welcome at the farm. Then she saw the Old Grange ringed in red, and at the same moment a flash of a woman's patterned silk dress crossed behind her eyes, making her heart do a weird little turn in her chest. That is where she would go, for starters, blindly and rather unreasoning. The car engine roared under the pressure of her foot and then she eased into reverse and backed out into the lane. The car was easier to handle than Dr Gray's old Mercedes had been. She quite enjoyed feeling wheels under her, again, and the old sureness returning to her hands as she carefully threaded her way through the early summer lanes the three miles to her destination.

The Old Grange was looking neglected and deserted, the garden even more overgrown than usual. Why had she come to an empty house? She drove right to the front door and looked round for a long time before unfastening her seat-belt and getting out to pause and ponder. It seemed to her the place was full of ghosts, it had never been one of her favourite calling places, and Lily's voice seemed to be teasing her from the undergrowth.

"I can thee you! You can't thee me! Play with me!"

"I can't, Lily," she heard herself answering automatically. "I have to give Pansy her injection. Be good, now!"

"Eh?" came a new voice. "Talking to yourself, Doctor?"

Old Mrs Jenkins had appeared shaking a blue-chequered duster.

"I'm sorry!" Nancy said quickly. "I didn't know anybody was in."

"Well, it does look a sorry place, doesn't it? I come in an' give things a wipe-over now and again. It's supposed to be wanted for a girls' finishing school, but it's greenbelt land, you see, and there would have to be a lot of building and extensions done. No private buyer would take it on. It hasn't even got central heating."

"It looks a sad, sorry place, Mrs Jenkins, and has some sad, sorry tales to tell."

"Aye. That was a sorry trip you took Miss Lily on, Doctor, and nearly finished you off, so I hear."

"Oh, I'm well enough, now. Do you remember that day, Mrs Jenkins?"

"Like it was yesterday. Miss Lily was so excited when I was packing up the picnic. She was a greedy girl, because she'd had a monstrous breakfast. I allus said she was too fat. She got cream all over her nice purple-flowered frock from poking her fingers in my bowl."

"I remember the flowers on her frock. Lily thought she looked very pretty."

This was a shot in the dark but Mrs Jenkins took it up.

"She spent more'n half an hour peeking in the mirror before you come. That vain she was. Then she was galumpin' up and down the stairs, askin' when you would be here."

"Well, I eventually arrived," Nancy

said with a rueful smile.

"Yes, you did. Right on time. So how come you never had the picnic, Doctor?"

"How do you know we didn't?"

Nancy was getting one of her headaches, again, but couldn't leave the matter alone. She knew, now, her visit here had not been without purpose, and meeting Mrs Jenkins had been pure luck, for the old woman had not been told she mustn't talk about the fateful day with the victim of it.

"Well, my son-in-law took me to see Lily in Burford, and she was full of her skinned knee when she fell out of the car, showing me the scars, and telling me how hungry she had been and you wouldn't stop to let her go to the lavatory. I know that young monkey. She would make any excuse to get to the eating part, but she said you were going to the deer park for the actual picnic. She tried to make you stop by pulling on the wheel but that you pushed her off and then grabbed her frock as she was falling."

Another flash behind Nancy's eyes and she saw quite clearly Lily Hulme's startled face going backwards through the car-door to the accompaniment of a scream and her own hand grabbing at a handful of purple floral material which made a small tearing sound and then disappeared from view.

The curtain was down again, now, but Nancy wasn't going to stop probing.

"So we didn't get to the deer park," she thought aloud.

"Obviously not, Doctor. You had your accident in Farmer Waley's bottom field. My son-in-law went along to help pull the car up on the verge, after the police and ambulance people had been and you and Lily had been taken away. They found the committal papers for Lily in the car, and the police took her to Burford. She was just crying and crying, shocked, I suppose."

"Yes, Mrs Jenkins. It was all very sad. But we must put it right behind

292

us, now. Well, I must leave you. I hope they do allow that girls' school here. It would be nice for them and the Old Grange would take on a new life."

She backed the car out into the lane, again, and consulted the map. Farmer Waley's land was marked in about four miles from the deer park where the picnic should have taken place. She drove down the lane slowly, looking to either side of her as Lily must have in her excitement of the occasion.

After about five miles of cruising a big bird suddenly swooped in front of the car and took off again.

"A heron!" Nancy cried out, and again the curtain behind her eyes was rent a little more.

"Ooh!" said a voice in her head. "A bird! A very big bird in that tree!"

"Sit back, Lily. It was probably a heron. Somebody round here has a pair comes every year — "

A blank, then, "I'm thtill hungry. Hurry up and thtop."

"You look for birds and squirrels on

293

your side. Tell me what you see but don't knock my arm."

Another blank.

"I'm nearly doing it Thtop! Thtop!"

"I can't in the middle of a lane on a bend. Just wait ten seconds."

"You're to thtop now, do you hear? I'll do it in your car."

Nancy physically had to hang on to the wheel, which was being pulled out of her control. She was amazed to find only her hands were upon it and she could manoeuvre easily enough. Then she turned her head and looked in horror at what was happening in her remembrance. She heard the click of Lily's seat-belt unfastening and saw the fat, frightened, blotchy face with its small, black eyes going backwards through the open passenger door with the heavy body after it accompanied by aloud, head-splitting scream.

Nancy stopped the car, trembling.

"So this must be where it happened," she decided, and looked about her. There was new fencing on her right joining up to older, weathered timbers. She left the car and walked up to the fence. The ground dropped into a growth of alder trees, the stout branch of one had been snapped clean off.

"That's what gave me the crack on the head," Nancy decided, and climbed the fence. As she walked down the decline she could clearly feel the car rocking under her, and Lily's screams behind yelling "Doctor! Doctor! Don't leave me! I'm hurt."

Every step she took was now accompanied by a vivid memory. The car was travelling sideways and didn't respond to the wheel. She reacted by turning the ignition off but couldn't find the brake to halt the vehicle. It was out of control, anyway, on the steep slope and would only have rolled. She felt the thud as the trees spun it round and the sharp lances of glass piercing her arms, she even heard an arm crunch as she shot through the windscreen and then there was an awful moment when she thought, 'I'll never see Don again,' before the mighty blow which felled her into blessed unconsciousness.

★ ★ ★

Don Wayne was surprised how many people had seen Nancy that afternoon. Mrs Gray had been surprised to see the young assistant in his car and going that way.

"Don't say she took the car without your knowing, Don?"

"No. I gave her permission to renew her driving licence. May I take the Traveller? I rather want to see that young lady."

"You don't even have to ask."

Mr Payne, working in his garden, had seen Doctor's car going in the direction of the Old Grange.

"There's nothin' else down that road now, Doctor, 'cept the canal. 'Oo were driving it, then?"

"My colleague, Dr Devine. Right then, Mr Payne. Don't overdo bending that back, now."

At the Old Grange Mrs Jenkins was just leaving, locking up the paint-flaking front door.

"My! Another visitor?"

"Actually, I have a message for Dr Devine. Have you seen her?"

"Why, yes, we had quite a long chat. We talked about that picnic which never come off. The day of the accident. You know?"

"I know only too well."

"Doctor looks very well, nowadays, a bit pale, maybe but we got to thank the good lord she's alive to tell the tale."

"Do you know which way she went?"

"Down the Burford road, I do believe. Yes. It was a red car. I saw it turn the corner."

"Thanks, Mrs Jenkins." He began to feel somewhat anxious. Nancy was obviously making the same journey as the one which had almost cost her her life. Obviously she was doing it to try to reclaim the slice of memory she had lost, but if she was unsuccessful, and today he refused to believe in miracles, then she would be even more depressed than heretofore. Rather than watch her blundering blindly about he had decided to tell her all he knew, and hope for a favourable, or at least a hopeful reaction from her. He had decided to follow in her tracks originally because he had forgotten to tell her his petrol gauge was not giving a true reading. Rather than have her stranded miles from anywhere he had to find her and put her wise to this defect.

He saw his car parked neatly on the verge about five miles down the Burford road. There was no one in it. He walked to the newly repaired fence and gazed down into the dell of alders. Was that a woman crying? He vaulted the fence and ran down the slope.

"Nancy! Nancy! What're you doing here? What's the matter?"

"Careful, Don," she sniffed as she sat on the grass. "I've just had a car accident."

Don automatically looked up at the

road and saw the roof of his red Volvo.

"It looked all right to me," he said. "What happened?"

"Oh, Don, you don't understand. I began to remember things. I saw a heron, and if that sounds disjointed there was a heron on the day of the accident, too. One thing led to another. Lily was with me in your car, and then I was here, and it all came back. I broke my arm again, smacked my silly head again, and there's no hole, any more, no more flashing lights of headaches. That's why I'm crying. I want to cry and cry."

"Why not?" he asked softly. "If it does you good — "

"May I do it in your arms."

He flung these members wide and hugged her to him. Her tears soaked his shirt and still she wept.

"It isn't the first time I've been here, is it?" she asked with a huge sniff.

"In this field? You know, now, it isn't."

"No. In your arms. I've remembered everything, Don. The way we were, the things we planned, your reasons for wanting to buy Crag Lee."

He held her the more tightly. He could scarcely believe he was hearing aright.

"I remembered we were in love, Don. I remembered the wonderful bits."

"Oh, my darling Nancy!"

"May I tell you something, Don? I never forgot I was in love with you. I have been almost since the beginning. But I had forgotten those ten wonderful days when you were in love with me."

"It wasn't only for ten days, Nancy. It was almost from the beginning with me, too. I couldn't see enough of you. I was afraid of sickening you, and I was quite prepared to knock Humphries down. You'll never know the self-control I had to exercise to even be polite to him."

"Oh, Don! I won't be leaving Greendales now, of course."

"That's good, because if you did I

was quite prepared to follow you. It would have been mightily inconvenient all round."

Suddenly she began to laugh, a little hysterically at first and then with her old, genuine mirth.

"Hold me closely just once more, Don, and then I suppose we'd better get back home. We'll be missed. Are — are you really happy?"

"I'm more than happy, Nancy. I'm ecstatic." He found her lips. They were warm and responsive and he knew this was the beginning for both of them of happy ever after. There were plans to be made, a wedding to arrange, but just for the moment the whole world was Nancy in his arms and loving him with her eloquent, soft brown eyes.

"Shall we go?" she asked him.

"Wherever thou goest," he quoted, and they both looked up as with a flapping of large wings a heron flew off towards the distant waters of the bay and the fish he knew were waiting to provide his supper.

## WITH SOMEBODY ELSE
### Theresa Charles

Rosamond sets off for Cornwall with Hugo to meet his family, blissfully unaware of the shocks in store for her.

## A SUMMER FOR STRANGERS
### Claire Hamilton

Because she had lost her job, her flat and she had no money, Tabitha agreed to pose as Adam's future wife although she believed the scheme to be deceitful and cruel.

## VILLA OF SINGING WATER
### Angela Petron

The disquieting incidents that occurred at the Vatican and the Colosseum did not trouble Jan at first, but then they became increasingly unpleasant and alarming.

## DOCTOR NAPIER'S NURSE
### Pauline Ash

When cousins Midge and Derry are entered as probationer nurses on the same day but at different hospitals they agree to exchange identities.


## A GIRL LIKE JULIE
### Louise Ellis

Caroline absolutely adored Hugh Barrington, but then Julie Crane came into their lives. Julie was the kind of girl who attracts men without even trying.


## COUNTRY DOCTOR
### Paula Lindsay

When Evan Richmond bought a practice in a remote country village he did not realise that a casual encounter would lead to the loss of his heart.

## ENCORE
### Helga Moray

Craig and Janet realise that their true happiness lies with each other, but it is only under traumatic circumstances that they can be reunited.

## NICOLETTE
### Ivy Preston

When Grant Alston came back into her life, Nicolette was faced with a dilemma. Should she follow the path of duty or the path of love?

## THE GOLDEN PUMA
### Margaret Way

Catherine's time was spent looking after her father's Queensland farm. But what life was there without David, who wasn't interested in her?

## HOSPITAL BY THE LAKE
### Anne Durham

Nurse Marguerite Ingleby was always ready to become personally involved with her patients, to the despair of Brian Field, the Senior Surgical Registrar, who loved her.

## VALLEY OF CONFLICT
### David Farrell

Isolated in a hostel in the French Alps, Ann Russell sees her fiancé being seduced by a young girl. Then comes the avalanche that imperils their lives.

## NURSE'S CHOICE
### Peggy Gaddis

A proposal of marriage from the incredibly handsome and wealthy Reagan was enough to upset any girl — and Brooke Martin was no exception.

## A DANGEROUS MAN
### Anne Goring

Photographer Polly Burton was on safari in Mombasa when she met enigmatic Leon Hammond. But unpredictability was the name of the game where Leon was concerned.

## PRECIOUS INHERITANCE
### Joan Moules

Karen's new life working for an authoress took her from Sussex to a foreign airstrip and a kidnapping; to a real life adventure as gripping as any in the books she typed.

## VISION OF LOVE
### Grace Richmond

When Kathy takes over the rundown country kennels she finds Alec Stinton, a local vet, very helpful. But their friendship arouses bitter jealousy and a tragedy seems inevitable.

## CRUSADING NURSE
### Jane Converse

It was handsome Dr. Corbett who opened Nurse Susan Leighton's eyes and who set her off on a lonely crusade against some powerful enemies and a shattering struggle against the man she loved.

## WILD ENCHANTMENT
### Christina Green

Rowan's agreeable new boss had a dream of creating a famous perfume using her precious Silverstar, but Rowan's plans were very different.

## DESERT ROMANCE
### Irene Ord

Sally agrees to take her sister Pam's place as La Chartreuse the dancer, but she finds out there is more to it than dyeing her hair red and looking like her sister.

## HEART OF ICE
### Marie Sidney

How was January to know that not only would the warmth of the Swiss people thaw out her frozen heart, but that she too would play her part in helping someone to live again?

## LUCKY IN LOVE
### Margaret Wood

Companion-secretary to wealthy gambler Laura Duxford, who lived in Monaco, seemed to Melanie a fabulous job. Especially as Melanie had already lost her heart to Laura's son, Julian.

## NURSE TO PRINCESS JASMINE
### Lilian Woodward

Nick's surgeon brother, Tom, performs an operation on an Arabian princess, and she invites Tom, Nick and his fiancé to Omander, where a web of deceit and intrigue closes about them.

## THE WAYWARD HEART
### Eileen Barry

Disaster-prone Katherine's nickname was "Kate Calamity", but her boss went too far with an outrageous proposal, which because of her latest disaster, she could not refuse.

## FOUR WEEKS IN WINTER
### Jane Donnelly

Tessa wasn't looking forward to meeting Paul Mellor again — she had made a fool of herself over him once before. But was Orme Jared's solution to her problem likely to be the right one?

## SURGERY BY THE SEA
### Sheila Douglas

Medical student Meg hadn't really wanted to go and work with a G.P. on the Welsh coast although the job had its compensations. But Owen Roberts was certainly not one of them!

## HEAVEN IS HIGH
### Anne Hampson

The new heir to the Manor of Marbeck had been found. But it was rather unfortunate that when he arrived unexpectedly he found an uninvited guest, complete with stetson and high boots.

## LOVE WILL COME
### Sarah Devon

June Baker's boss was not really her idea of her ideal man, but when she went from third typist to boss's secretary overnight she began to change her mind.

## ESCAPE TO ROMANCE
### Kay Winchester

Oliver and Jean first met on Swale Island. They were both trying to begin their lives afresh, but neither had bargained for complications from the past.

## CASTLE IN THE SUN
### Cora Mayne

Emma's invalid sister, Kym, needed a warm climate, and Emma jumped at the chance of a job on a Mediterranean island. But Emma soon finds that intrigues and hazards lurk on the sunlit isle.

## BEWARE OF LOVE
### Kay Winchester

Carol Brampton resumes her nursing career when her family is killed in a car accident. With Dr. Patrick Farrell she begins to pick up the pieces of her life, but is bitterly hurt when insinuations are made about her to Patrick.

## DARLING REBEL
### Sarah Devon

When Jason Farradale's secretary met with an accident, her glamorous stand-in was quite unable to deal with one problem in particular.

# THE PRICE OF PARADISE
## Jane Arbor

It was a shock to Fern to meet her estranged husband on an island in the middle of the Indian Ocean, but to discover that her father had engineered it puzzled Fern. What did he hope to achieve?

# DOCTOR IN PLASTER
## Lisa Cooper

When Dr. Scott Sutcliffe is injured, Nurse Caroline Hurst has to cope with a very demanding private case. But when she realises her exasperating patient has stolen her heart, how can Caroline possibly stay?

# A TOUCH OF HONEY
## Lucy Gillen

Before she took the job as secretary to author Robert Dean, Cadie had heard how charming he was, but that wasn't her first impression at all.

## ROMANTIC LEGACY
### Cora Mayne

As kenr maid the Armstrongs, Ann Brown, had no idea that she would become the central figure in a web of mystery and intrigue.

## THE RELENTLESS TIDE
### Jill Murray

Steve Palmer shared Nurse Marie Blane's love of the sea and small boats. Marie's other passion was her step-brother. But when danger threatened who should she turn to — her step-brother or the man who stirred emotions in her heart?

## ROMANCE IN NORWAY
### Cora Mayne

Nancy Crawford hopes that her visit to Norway will help her to start life again. She certainly finds many surprises there, including unexpected happiness.